Happy

or

Otherwise

2-12-07

Stories by
Diana Joseph

[signature: Diana Joseph]

Carnegie Mellon University Press
Pittsburgh, Pennsylvania 2003

For Cathy,
Wishing you much happy
and hardly any otherwise
—Best
Diana

Acknowledgments

I owe endless gratitude to my friend Melanie Rae Thon, for her support and encouragement. Thank you, too, to Allen Learst, reader, publicist and guitar player extraordinaire.

The stories in this collection originally appeared in the following publications:

Threepenny Review, "Bloodlines"
Beloit Fiction Journal, "Naming Stories"
Gulf Coast, "Windows and Words"
Mid-American Review, "Approximate to Salvation"
Puerto del Sol, "Sick Child"
Indiana Review, "Expatriates"
Weber Studies, "The Fifth Mrs. Hughes"
William and Mary Review, "Schandorsky's Mother"
Colorado Review, "Many Will Enter, Few Will Win"
South Dakota Review, "If I Close Them"
Cimarron Review, "Shared and Stolen"

Book Design by Andrea Georgiana and Julia Moran

Library of Congress Control Number 2002115405
ISBN 0087483968
Copyright 2003 by Diana Josephs
All Rights Reserved
Printed and Bound in the United States of America
10 9 8 7 6 5 4 3 2 1

If parental behavior consists of nothing more than refraining from eating the children, no great emotional drama is necessary. But to feed them, wash them, and risk your life for them – or (perhaps even harder) to let them chew on you, to let them snatch your dinner, and to put up with their noise – you had better love them deeply, at least for the time being.

Jeffrey Moussaieff Masson and Susan McCarthy
When Elephants Weep: The Emotional Lives of Animals

For Clayton

Contents

11	Bloodlines
20	Naming Stories
32	Windows and Words
46	Approximate to Salvation
69	Sick Child
82	Expatriates
100	The Fifth Mrs. Hughes
114	Schandorsky's Mother
135	Many Will Enter, Few Will Win
152	If I Close Them
168	What Remains
185	Shared and Stolen

Bloodlines

My father was a tall man, and when he was young, he'd been whip-skinny. Now his stomach pouched out – hard fat – and his arms were thick and strong from pounding nails into horses' feet. Horses were his passion. He was partial to Appaloosas, a flashy breed, those loud spots. He liked to look out the window and watch them grazing in the pasture – green grass, blue sky, spotted horses. When they ate the grass down to stubble, he stretched a rope across the lane and let them graze in the pasture. He liked to look out the window and see a horse looking back in.

For a few hours each afternoon, my father let the Quarter Horse stud out of its dark stall and put it in the southern pasture. There was an oak tree growing in the middle of the pasture, and the stud was killing it, chewing off the bark and gnawing right into the trunk. Horses will do that sort of thing when they get bored: chew on trees, crib wood fences, jerk down their feed buckets. It gets to be a habit for them, but one you forgive – like smoking.

Sometimes, my father propped me on a wood fence, leaning his body against mine so his left hand was free to hold his cigarette, and his right hand was free to offer half an apple to a horse. He blew smoke into the horse's face until it sneezed and I laughed. *Tabby Cat*, he'd say, *someday, you're going to ride a horse.*

In western Pennsylvania, August is a humid month. The humidity wraps its sticky arms around you and licks the back of your neck – that damp place under your hair. We lived on forty-seven acres. We had horses and dogs. We had a barn that my father built.

My father hunted white tail buck. When he was fifteen, he killed a twelve point. Its head hung on a wall in our living room. Its eyes were made of glass. The gun that killed it was in the living room, encased in wood and glass.

The gun in the barn was meant for killing large rats and stray dogs, fearless raccoons with foaming mouths; my father kept it hung on the wall next to the saddles and bridles and bits. He was a steady shot.

Horses fall hard when they are shot. Stall boards splinter and crack, give in to their weight. Dust rises out of their coats. Their eyes stay open.

On a Saturday morning in August, my brother died, and my father shot every horse in the barn: five Appaloosa mares, one Quarter Horse stud, one paint pony – seven bullets. He hurled his gun across the fence, into the pasture, and he took off running, his steps high and clean, graceful – as if he'd practiced running like that.

As if he knew where he was going.

That afternoon, men and boys who knew my father and my brother came to our farm. I stood at the high window in my parents' bedroom, my chin level with the ledge, my mother just inches away, but still out of reach, as she wept quietly into the telephone. She was calling people and telling them that Martin had died, Martin was dead. She was sitting on the edge of her bed, her eyes were closed, and as she talked, she rubbed her fingers in tight circles like she did when she had a headache.

I stayed at the window. I watched those men and boys walk up the lane. Loggers and Amish Dutch farmers, high school football players, mechanics and carpenters. They carried chain saws and crowbars, hammers and rope. They pried off and cut through siding boards to tear down the walls of the barn. They wrapped rope around dead horses' stiff legs and dragged them out of their stalls, trailing blood and flies. One man hitched the paint pony's legs to my father's tractor and pulled it out. *Rigor mortis*, he said. Another man knew a guy who worked for the county and convinced him to bring their backhoe. None of them seemed to know where my father had gone or when he'd be back, but it didn't really matter. They were still going to bury those horses.

Earlier that summer, my mother waved a hair brush at me, and I backed into a corner like I was terribly afraid of her. I wasn't, of course; I was just showing off for my father. *I'm good and sick of fooling with you, Tabbitha*, she said, but I slipped past her, hiking up my nightgown so I wouldn't trip. *I don't want you to brush my hair*, I told her. *I want that guy* – I was pointing at my father – *I want him to do it.*

And he did. He unwound my braid and gently brushed out my hair, counting off every stroke, one to one hundred and one, unlike my mother, who cheated, skipping numbers as if I wouldn't notice.

My brother had a wavy mop of uncontrollable hair. He wanted his bangs to cover his forehead so he tried to tame them by holding them down with pieces of masking tape. He came into the kitchen like this on the morning he died. My mother put down her coffee cup. *Come with me*, she told him. She led him into the bathroom, and when they came back out, the masking tape was gone, Martin's bangs laid flat and heavy, and he smelled like Aqua Net.

That summer, something mysterious was happening to the drinking glasses. They kept breaking, clean breaks that snapped away from the rims. We didn't know it at the time, but it was my mother's ring. When her soapy hand circled the inside of the glass, the diamond cut through.

My mother's ring was a present from my

father: a diamond fifteen years too late. It was a guilt gift: my father bought the Quarter Horse stud without telling her he was going to.

My mother didn't love horses. Not the way they smell – of sweat and hay and manure. Not the way they buck and snort, the way they chew on your leather shoestrings. She didn't love the way their hair drifts across the floor in the barn, is carried by a breeze through the air, is brought into the house on your clothes. She was afraid of horses. When my father was in the barn, she stayed in the kitchen. Maybe she looked out the window, toward the barn, full of longing. Was she remembering the woods, making love with my father on his deer stand – before horses became his passion? Did she hold a glass under steaming water, tap it lightly against the faucet, and wonder why it cracked?

She loved my father. These are the things she would forgive him for: head of a buck suspended on the wall, calloused fingers snagging her green silk blouse, son conceived on a deer stand.

She said, *Men will only be as good as you let them.*

My brother and I watched my father work the Quarter Horse stud. He put it in the cross ties and touched it: pinching its nose, lifting each leg, rubbing its belly. He put it on a lunge line and ran it in tight circles. Left, then right, then left again, flicking the whip at its feet. My father beat the Quarter Horse stud: with the handle of a pitchfork, his whip, a branch from an oak tree. The stud backed into a corner of its stall and trembled at the sight of my father but it never looked away from him.

My father laughed. *He thinks he's a tough guy*, he said. *He thinks he's tougher than me. But watch this: I can move him with my head.*

When he tilted his head to the left, the stud stepped left; he tilted right, and the stud stepped right.

How'd you do that? my brother said. *Will he do it for me?*

My father said, *Only for me. It's because he hates me.*

My father and brother bickered over whether I should have a pony or a small horse. Martin thought ponies were short on patience and full of spite. *Ponies bite*, he said. *They kick. A pony will throw her off first chance it gets.*

Who are you? my father asked. *Sir Knows-a-lot?*

My brother loved horses, but he wasn't a good rider. He didn't trust a horse when he was on its back. I never saw him ride anyone but Colter, my paint pony, a gelding, fat and stubborn. Martin had to help me saddle him: Colter had a habit of puffing himself up as soon as he felt the weight of the saddle. The minute Martin cinched the girth, Colter relaxed, exhaling noisily, causing the saddle to slide loose. *Goddamn pony*, he'd mutter. He'd ride poor Colter hard, snapping the reins against his neck and hips until white sweat lathered up. By the time I got on Colter, he was too exhausted to give me any trouble.

Twenty years since I've been on a horse, but I'm still a good rider.

You don't forget.

On the Saturday morning in late August that my brother died, my father got up late. After French toast and sausage links and silence that lasted until he drank several cups of coffee and smoked two cigarettes, he asked my mother if she knew what Martin's plans for the day were. She was washing breakfast dishes. She said, *He's in the barn.* My father said, *I've got fence post holes I want him to dig.* He let the screen door swing shut behind him, not bothering to close the heavy door – it was a morning cool for August, but it would get warmer and eventually hot, humid – and the dogs were barking, and you could hear country music coming from the barn radio, and a horse was kicking against its stall, and a horse whinnied, and the others answered, and when my father came back, he stood outside the door and shouted through the screen: *Call an ambulance!*

My mother didn't hear him. She was stooped over, dumping wet coffee grounds into the plastic bucket she kept under the sink – she spread all sorts of scraps over her tomatoes. *What?* she said.

Don't ask me what. Do it. Call the ambulance.

Then he was gone.

He'd found Martin in the barn. Martin in a stall, gate slid shut. The Quarter Horse stud standing on his arm. The Quarter Horse stud putting back its ears and showing its teeth. The rising smell of piss, the dogs' pink tongues, a steel guitar solo, and Martin already dead. Kicked and stepped on. Already dead. When the ambulance arrived, my father had the stud horse in the cross ties, and with cracks of his whip, he'd bloodied its nose and belly and legs and ass and genitals.

I counted seven shots.

Through a window, I watched my father run, becoming very small.

Where was he going?

My mother said she didn't know.

Then she said, *You want your dad?*

The keys to his truck were on top of the refrigerator; she took them.

She said, *Let's go get him, Tabbitha.*

She knew exactly where to go. She drove down the lane, turning left onto Bowden Road, another left onto a dirt road that led us through neighboring hayfields. When the dirt road ended, we got out and walked. Neither of us said anything. Mosquitoes swarmed thick in the air; crickets were chirping; that eerie purple-gold dusk streaked across the sky, and every time you blinked, the sun dropped a little further. Our shadows were long and narrow. We found him sitting on a hickory stump under his deer stand, his elbows were resting on his thighs, his hands were covering his ears, he was looking at the space between his feet, and I have seen men sitting this way since – in airports and bus stops and train stations, at this very moment on the edge of my bed; men broken by bankruptcy and faithless wives and their children's hate – and I hate when men sit so huddled and hidden and defeated. Men will only be as strong as you let them. When my father looked up, he said, *I knew you'd find me. I knew you'd come.*

Naming Stories

Sometimes, I told this story: I was conceived at Woodstock, in the rain, the music, the mud, on the night of a full moon. So my hippie mother named me Diana after the Roman goddess of the moon. No one was as impressed with this story as I was. Especially not my mother. In 1969, she was wearing bell bottoms, and she might have smoked pot a time or two – which was about as hippie as one could get in western Pennsylvania – but she'd never been to Woodstock. She never spent a night outside New Castle. She told me that my name came out of a romance novel she read when she was thirteen. "I want you to quit making things up," she said. "It's embarrassing."

I am my mother's first child, and as mothers will do for their first born, my mother kept a Baby Book about me. It's all there, faithfully recorded, the history of my infant self. First step, first tooth, first word. There's a sealed envelope containing strands from my first haircut. There's a heading that reads, *Looks Like*, and under that heading, there's a sentence that someone scribbled out. Next to that sentence, someone wrote, "A little red potato."

In fifth grade, in science class, a unit on genetics. Mrs. Lane says that brown eyes are a dominant gene while blue eyes are recessive. Blue-eyed parents, she says, will always have blue-eyed children.

I argue with her about this. I insist that she's mistaken, misinformed, just flat out wrong. "No way," I say, and I tell her why. My mother has blue eyes, my father has blue eyes. Both of my brothers have eyes that are blue. But not me. My eyes are brown.

Two years pass before I mention this to my parents. It's Report Card Day, and I've failed math. I need a way to distract them.

It works.

Diana. Dianna. Dyana. Dina. Deana. Deanna. Deanne. Diane. Dianne. Dyan. Dee. Di. Dy. In school, in math class, daydreaming. Trying out new names, different spellings. I jumped out of my skin when Mr. Sarbo said, "Diameter."

In New Castle, Pennsylvania, there was a Stewart Diana. Occasionally, I got his mail. There was also another Diana Stewart. Once, the police came to my door looking for her: she'd rented a camcorder and a VCR and never returned them. Penn Power refused to give me service unless I could prove that I wasn't the Diana Stewart who skipped out on a twelve-hundred dollar electric bill.

Another time, I got a collect call from the Lawrence County Jail – an inmate looking for Diana Stewart. "C'mon, sweetness," he said. "Don't do me this way. I know it's you." He was hoping that his Diana Stewart, a girl he'd met in a bar, would post his bail.

Of course, it wasn't me.

In bars, at bowling alleys, at concerts and parties, smoky places, licking salt off a man's palm, squirts of lemon juice, shots of tequila, drinking beer and smoking pot, I gave men fake names. In Youngstown, Ohio, at Kassie's Back Road Lounge, a man was insisting that he knew me, he recognized me, he'd be able to place me as soon as he heard my name. He had a Superman tattoo and his nose looked like it had been shaped with putty. I told him that my name was Susan B. Anthony, and that I was from Seneca Falls, New York. "I knew it," he cried. "I knew I knew you!"

Report Card Day, seventh grade. I failed math. I know I'm in trouble, and I'm looking for a way to stall. I hand my parents my report card, and say, "Am I adopted?" I don't really think I am.

But after much crying and stroking my cheek, my hair, hugging me too long, too close, and too tight, I get the story: my mother is my mother, but my father is not my father. He adopted me, he gave me his name. "It's a good name," my mother tells me. "You should be proud."

But who is my father?

Naming Stories

She says, "He's just a man I used to know."

But what's his name?

She says, "I don't remember, and it's not really all that important anyhow."

Does he know about me, does he want to see me?

My mother says, "I wouldn't dwell on this." She smiles and says, "I wouldn't waste my time thinking about it if I were you."

Three children called my mother Mom. She was in the bathroom, and we'd pound on the door. Mom, Mom. She was on the telephone, and we'd demand her attention. Mom, Mom. She was in the basement, sorting laundry, and we'd stand at the top of the steps, hollering, Mom, Mom.

My mother never said she was going to sell us to the gypsies, but she did threaten to move away and change her name.

My mother is blonde, and blue-eyed, and fair-skinned. I am brunette, and brown-eyed, and olive-skinned. People have told me that I resemble her – *You are your mother's child* – and I look and look and look, and I can't see it. But here's one thing: there's a certain way my mother will smile when someone has said something that she finds disagreeable, but still feels obligated to respond to. I have that same smile. And here's another: we both had a child with men we didn't marry.

*

In high school, I worked the circulation desk at the New Castle Public Library. I argued with the head librarian about how unnecessary it was for me to wear a name tag. "The patrons don't need to know my name," I said. "I don't want them to know my name." The patrons liked the library because it was heated in the winter and air-conditioned in the summer. On my name tag, I wrote "Melanie-Margaret." I spoke with a southern accent and pretended to be a girl from a Tennessee Williams play. When the head librarian heard a man say, "Thank you, Melanie-Margaret," she ripped the tag from my shirt. "You are exempt," she said.

I've always wanted a nickname. My youngest brother has one. After he was potty trained, he'd flush the toilet and wave bye-bye. So we started calling him Bye-Bye. My brother played high school football, and when he felt like it, he could run faster than anyone else on the field. The *New Castle News* ran headlines: "Stewart Waves Bye-Bye." My brother has a reputation among the female population of western Pennsylvania: Bye-Bye Stewart, Heartbreaker.

This is the pet name of my childhood: Diana Banana. My mother called me that. My brother Jimmy, who used to be James, called me Potato Head. One of the neighborhood boys called me Double D. When we were in love, my husband called me Sugar Bear. When we were estranged, my husband called me Bitch, Slut, Whore. "I feel sorry for you," my husband said, "because I don't think you know yourself." He said, "Sweetheart." He said, "Darling." He called me his Beautiful Brown-Eyed Girl. He said, "You're full of shit clear up to your eyes and that's the reason they're brown."

Sometimes, I told this story: my mother was madly in love with a handsome brown-eyed boy who, unfortunately, got drafted and sent off to the jungles of Vietnam. He died there, a tragic death, and though my mother ended up married to this other guy, she never forgot her one true love, my father, the poor dead solider, whose name is etched on a black wall in Washington D.C.

I asked my mother if she'd ever dated a boy who'd been sent to Vietnam. I thought I was terribly clever and sly.

"Probably," she said.

"Were you madly in love with him?"

"Oh, love," she said, flatly. "I was madly in love with all my boyfriends. I was in love with anyone who might take me out of New Castle. That's before I understood that love is liquid." She smiled. "It takes the shape of whatever container you put it in."

Darryl, Art, Mike, Pat. Mike, Paul, Tom, Shawn. Chris. Todd. Darren. Mark. Rex. Tod. Scooter. Micky. Ricardo. Gary. I've had many lovers, too many to remember all of their names. I'm twenty-five years old, I've been having sex since

I was fifteen, I don't like doing the math.

What I'm left with are their actions. That guy who played in a band. That guy who voted for Ronald Reagan, twice. The sweaty guy who wanted to open the window even though it was late December. The one I cheated on my husband with. The one who cried because what he really wanted was to be a priest. The one who is my child's father. The one who was someone else's father.

After I turned eighteen, I strayed from home, far enough to be long-distance from my mother, but not so far that I couldn't pick up a weather report for New Castle on my car radio. Wheeling, West Virginia. East Liverpool, Ohio. Bradford, Pennsylvania. I was a waitress, I sold water filters and vacuum cleaners, I cleaned hotel rooms. I'd wake up in hotel rooms, feeling abandoned, and I'd reach across the strange man asleep beside me. I'd reach for the phone book, and I'd look to see who else has my name.

Then I'd look up the name of my biological father. It was all I knew about him, that, and the color of his eyes, which I knew must be brown. I'd hand over change to the guy in the toll booth, I'd let a guy in a bar light my cigarette, I'd brush hair off my lover's forehead, looking closely at the color of his eyes.

The man I married is named Gary, and at this historical moment, men named Gary are in their forties, approaching fifty. A heart murmur kept him out of Vietnam. I kept my maiden name. A lot of people – family, friends, my mother – had a problem with this. "When you get married," they said, "two people become as one. Sharing a name symbolizes this."

But I was stubborn. Not only did I want my name for personal reasons, reasons that had to do with me becoming someone's wife, making it imperative that I maintain some of my original identity, but also for reasons that had to do with sheer laziness and not wanting to stand in line at the Department of Motor Vehicles. "I really like the driver's license picture I have for Diana Stewart," I explained.

My mother's solution to this was to call me by my husband's name anyway. She addressed my birthday cards using his name. She introduced me to people using his name. One Christmas, she gave us plane tickets, a trip to Mexico, my ticket in his name, which caused enormous problems during check-in when an airline official asked me for ID.

I called my mother from the airport. "A simple question," I said. "What's my name?"

She sighed. She said, "You tell me."

At fifteen, I learn the name of my biological father. It's because I'm in trouble – again – and again, I'm looking for a way to change the subject. My mother's eyes can be remarkably blue, especially when they are wet. "He's just a man I used to know," she says. "Daddy has been your father in every way that counts."

My father – not my biological father – but the man I called Daddy when I was a little girl, the man I call Dad now, the man who raised me and gave me his name – his first name is Michael. I named my son after him. He is a good man, decent; he claimed me as his own.

There were times, though, when I was angry with him, and I'd look at him and think, *You're not my father. I don't have to listen to you.*

I've wondered about times when he was angry with me, if he's ever looked at me only to see the dark eyes of another man staring back.

Absence makes that other man perfect. I can make him into whatever I want him to be. I can make him call me Princess. I can make him into a presence watching me from afar, waiting for me to recognize him. I imagine that he follows behind me to ensure that I'm not kidnapped walking to school, and I believe that when we find each other, he's going to dismember any man who tries to hurt me. He's going to kill any man who tries to touch me, and I'm going to let him.

I'm fifteen years old and demanding to know my father's name. It starts out as a diversion – *So what I was out past curfew, that's not what matters, what matters is it's my right to know who my father is, tell me his name* – until my mother says, "He's here. In New Castle."

She says, "Daddy and I thought about moving away from here, but you'd still have to know."

She says, "You don't want to go look him

up, Kiddo, trust me. You won't like what you find."

She says, "He doesn't deserve you."

Then she told me his name.

Just that once, my mother said my biological father's name. I never asked her to say it again. I've never forgotten the name she told me, but sometimes, I wonder if I heard her right. Sometimes, I'm not sure she was telling me the truth, that the name she gave me is indeed his name. A character on Sesame Street, a puppet who is a magician, has the very same name, and it would be just like my mother to play that sort of prank.

She told me his name, and then she said, "Ask me. Whatever you want to know, I'll tell you."

This is what she told me: he failed Senior Math; he's an alcoholic; when his draft number was called, he was twenty years old and still in high school; he told her to get an abortion. Everything else I wanted to know – his birthday, his height, his middle name – she said she couldn't remember.

Years later, my mother would tell me that memory is a liquid. I'd been in labor for thirty-six hours before I shoved out a son. My mother was holding him, trying to convince me that I'd forget the pain. "Memory is fluid," she said. "It takes the shape of whatever container you put it in."

"I thought that was love," I said.

"What's the difference?" she said. "They're equally unreliable."

New Castle, Pennsylvania. It's an old steel mill town. It calls itself the Fireworks Capital of the World. Boys in New Castle are named Tony and Vito; girls answer to Tiffany and Stephanie. If you want a job working for the city, your last name has to end in a vowel. Years of drifting brought me back. I had a child now, and I still had to know.

A hotel room, a bed, the middle of the night. My son is with my parents, asleep in the house where I grew up. I'm with a man. Like so many of my lovers, this man is old enough to be my father. He's tall and thin, small-boned, and the hair on his head is dark brown, while his chest hair and pubic hair is gray – I think he must color his hair – and he has brown, brown eyes. He tells me that he was in Vietnam on the day I was born. In fact, he says, he very well might have a child, one about my age, in Phu Bai, a strange place between the Central Highlands and the South China Sea.

"If it was a boy," my lover says, "its name is Bernard. The mother was part French. I don't know what she called it if it was a girl."

Doesn't he want to know?

My lover says, "No, not really. That was a long time ago. Ancient history."

I smile at this. I can't help it. It's that smile of my mother's, somewhere between condescending and absurd. While he's making love to me, I'm smiling, I'm thinking, *Who is this man?* I think of my son, his brown eyes, his unknown father, the wonder of looking at him and seeing my own face

Naming Stories

across time and gender. He's what I would have looked like if I had been a boy. My mother once told me that if I had been a boy, she would have named me after her father whose name I don't know. My lover tastes like Scotch and cigarettes, and beside the bed, on the nightstand, there's a phone book, *New Castle, Pennsylvania and Surrounding Areas*, and after he falls asleep, I stretch across him, reaching for it, afraid of what I'll find.

What will I find?

His name, his number, his address.

Will I call?

Yes.

What will happen?

A sleepy girl will answer. She'll say, *Hello, hello, hello?* then, *Who is this?* and I'll hear a man's voice say, *Who is it?* then, *Just hang up,* and the girl will say, *Fuck you, pervert,* and that's when I'll put down the phone.

Sometimes, I'll tell this story: I called my father in the middle of the night, and a sleepy girl answered. This girl was not my father's young wife, and she was not his teenage lover, and she wasn't some whore he brought home for the night. She was his daughter, my sister. A fifth grader with pig tails. Good at math. Brunette and brown-eyed. When she said, *Hello,* I apologized for waking her, and I told her I was sorry for bothering her, and she told me I didn't wake her at all, she was up in the kitchen, having a drink of water, and when a man's voice, my father's, said, *Who is it?* she handed him the phone, saying, *Diana.*

Windows and Words

On a drunken sloshy night, Leslie used a toothpick to spear chunks of pineapple out of a tub filled with grain punch. The pineapple was stained a deep purple color; her tongue and the insides of her cheeks were stained deep purple. Leslie ate the pineapple, then allowed a philosophy major to thrust up against her. When he said, "There's a hole in the crotch of your pants," Leslie told him, "Window to the world."

The philosophy major was lanky and pale and appealing in a needs-a-bath sort of way. His hair was too long, and when he finally did go to the barber, he got it cut too short. Sex with him was lots of fun: he used philosophy as a form of foreplay. Nietzsche was a favorite of his, and as he made love, he'd whisper from *Thus Spake Zarathustra* – something about how men long for both danger and play, something about how women should be dangerous playthings.
Leslie found herself smitten to say the least.

*

Leslie had a recurring dream. She dreamed of the wicked whore of Babylon. The wicked whore was an enormous woman with heaving breasts and a huge red mouth and fluttery eyelashes. Leslie dreamed that the wicked whore was parading through town on horseback, laughing and peeking in everyone's windows. She told the philosophy major about it. When he laughed, and said, "You have a great imagination," Leslie slugged him, and made him tell her something.

He told her about his parents' divorce when he was five, how after his father left, his mother would slip into bed with him and curl herself around him. "It got to where I couldn't sleep without her," he said. "Then she got remarried, which was terrible. I used to sleep on the floor outside their bedroom."

Leslie thought this was sweet. She thought the philosophy major was needy and vulnerable, and she mistook this for love.

He played his guitar for her.
He read his poems.
He said he couldn't sleep without her.

She typed his papers for him. He didn't know the difference between a colon and a semi-colon, but Leslie didn't point this out. She just fixed it.

When toothbrushes went on sale – buy-one-get-one-free – she gave him one.

She did his laundry.

Leslie didn't mind doing any of these things one bit: it reminded her of her mother, slipping a spoonful of Fiber Con into her dad's iced tea.

Through a window, Leslie and the philosophy major watched leaves falling, rain falling, snow falling.

One of them said, "I love you."

The other said, "I love you, too."

Was it the sex?

The sex was part of it. Leslie still confused sex with love. She still thought sex was just a reason to look into someone's eyes, sex was just a reason to remember the color of someone's eyes.

On the sagging mattress above their heads, the philosophy major's roommate slept or pretended to sleep. The roommate ignored the philosophy major's whispering; he ignored all the passionate racket Leslie was making. The roommate tossed and turned a lot, and from Leslie's perspective – under the mattress, under the philosophy major – the tossing and turning brought to mind a baby rolling about in the womb. Sometimes, she could make out body parts: a pointy elbow, the flat sole of a foot, rounded buttocks.

Windows and Words

This is what Leslie's desire was like: babysitting a child up past his bedtime. He keeps asking the same question, over and over: *Can I? Can I?* She's trying to read a book, write a paper, figure out what "postmodern" means, but this kid won't leave her alone. He's pesky, but charming.

Acting on desire, Leslie thought, is just another way to procrastinate.

Soon, Leslie wasn't feeling so hot: tired, nauseous, very moody. She went to the student health center where the nurse slid a thermometer under her tongue and asked for the date of her last period. This was something Leslie had to think about because she couldn't remember the date of her last period. But she wasn't about to tell the nurse that. Instead, Leslie told her that it had been exactly a week since her last period, and she said she was suddenly feeling much better, and she asked, "Can I please go now?"

Leslie may have been smitten with the philosophy major, but she wasn't thrilled about the prospect of having his baby. She was an English major, about to graduate, and she had plans – undefined, unknown, unspoken plans – but plans, nonetheless.

Mostly, she had the word "plans."

There's another word she could have had, one that is synonymous with "freedom." She repeated this word, silently, to herself. Each time she did, the wicked whore of Babylon appeared. She was still enormous, still laughing, still peeking in windows, but this time, the windows she was peeking in were Leslie's.

Her mother said, "This is what you want" Runny noses and chocolate chip cookies? I thought you were smarter than that."

Her father said, "Forty thousand dollars. Your education cost me forty thousand dollars. You owe me forty thousand dollars."

The philosophy major's mother was on her third husband, and she had a new baby of her own. She had advice about breast-feeding. "Electric pumps," she said.

His father had an empty double-wide on a lot outside town. "Rent free," he said. "Until you kids get on your feet."

Four months were what it took for Leslie and the philosophy major to move the word "marry" from an agreement into an action. To execute the word "marry." When she married him, he was no longer a philosophy major: he'd graduated from college, and he was now an unemployed philosopher moonlighting as a lumberjack for the sawmill his father owned. The lumberjack's hair hung over his collar, he wore steel-toed boots, and the beard he grew made him look dangerous and appealing.

When he married Leslie, she was no longer a dangerous plaything with the word "plans." She'd graduated from college, and she was seven months pregnant. She was a mind trailing behind a stomach. She was a stomach that old ladies in grocery stores felt free to stroke and pat. She cut her hair chin-length. She wore breathable cotton and rubber-soled shoes. The panic in her eyes when old ladies patted The Stomach made her look dangerous and anti-maternal.

Leslie longed to use The Stomach as a weapon, a brutal weapon; she longed to knock old ladies in grocery stores over with it, knock them out of the way, knock them into pyramids of tomato paste cans and watch it all come crashing down.

They were married at Pauline Isaac's Wedding Chapel and Motel. The Reverend Stanley J. Turner and his wife were the only attendants. Before getting started, Reverend Turner presented an option: "Do you want the simple ceremony or the fancy one?"

What was the difference?

"Lit candles," said Reverend Turner. "But they cost an extra five dollars."

The lumberjack squeezed Leslie's hand. "We'll take it," he said.

When Mrs. Turner pressed a button on a

tape recorder, *The Wedding March* played.

Now Leslie was a wife. But she wondered: what is a wife?

She thought hard. She tried to remember the wives she'd seen, the wives she'd known: how did they behave?

Was a wife someone who, upon hearing her husband say, "Working men need lemonade and lots of it," pours him a frosted glass?

That was something she'd seen on *The Brady Bunch.*

Was a wife someone who, upon hearing her husband say, "Come talk to me while I take a shit," follows him into the bathroom?

That was something her dad said; it was something her mother did.

Was a wife someone who had sex with her husband?

But Leslie felt too pregnant to be touched.

When the lumberjack hooked his leg over hers in bed one night, she told him, "We have yet to consummate this marriage."

He said, "I know, I know."

She said, "That means we can still get it annulled." She smiled at his sweet, worried face. "Just kidding," she said.

Through a window, Leslie and the lumberjack watched robins pulling up worms, sparrows pecking at the ground. They watched a hummingbird, tiny wings fluttering; it hovered, then slammed hard against the glass.

    One of them said, "I love you."

    The other said, "I love you, too."

    This is what Leslie was thinking: "Was it sex I enjoyed or sex I endured that got me in this situation?"

    She cleaned. Compulsively. Dusting, vacuuming, washing the sticky paneled walls. Washing the grimy windows. She put doilies everywhere and covered the grubby couch with a floral bedspread. The lumberjack was amused. "You're nesting," he said.

    His days were spent in the woods. He cut down trees and skidded logs. His father paid him fifty dollars a day. There was a drugstore he passed on the way home from the woods, and a bakery, and a gas station, and he stopped and bought cigarettes, cookies, cakes, motor oil.

    One day, the lumberjack spent his last five dollars on a pack of Camels, eight fudge brownies, and a loaf of white bread. By morning, the brownies were gone. Leslie was crying. She said, "I ate them all. Every single one of them." She said, "I hate my life."

    The lumberjack tried to comfort her. He thought she was worried about money. When he said, "Brownies will get you through times of no money better than money will get you through times of no brownies," Leslie pushed him away. She said, "What the hell is that? Your new philosophy?"

There was a pair of denim maternity overalls. She wore them every day.

There were large vitamins. She gagged swallowing them.

There were words to think, but not to say: "plans"; "trapped"; "constipation."

On the way home from the woods, the lumberjack stopped at the drugstore and bought more vitamins and books about babies: *Your Baby, Your Child; What to Expect When You're Expecting; 1,001 Names for Baby*.

He read them; she didn't.

There was a long dark line creeping up the center of The Stomach. It divided her in half.

There were deep purple stretch marks zigzagging across this line.

There were more words to think without speaking: "resentment"; "motherhood."

Leslie longed to lie face down. She dozed but didn't sleep. She paced, wobbly. She lit up a Camel and blew smoke out the window, tapping ashes through the hole in the screen. The lumberjack slept on his stomach. The lumberjack's baby rolled about impatiently. Leslie eased herself into bed, flat on her back. She amused herself by placing the pack of Camels on The Stomach and watching it kick them off.

>Leslie gave birth.
>To a perfectly formed daughter.
>A perfect daughter who emerged from her womb with the umbilical cord wrapped tightly around her neck. She didn't move. She didn't cry. She was blue, her skin was a pale blue, and someone said, *I'm sorry*.

>Leslie refused the sedative, the Tylenol. She refused all medication offered to her. She wanted to feel this pain. She thought she didn't deserve relief from it.

>The day after Leslie gave birth, the lumberjack brought her home from the hospital. This was the day her milk came in. Her breasts were rigid and hard, hot, enormous. Her breasts hurt. Her nipples, stretched nearly flat, were a deep purple color. It hurt to wear a bra. It hurt to wear a shirt. She sat on the rocking chair, naked from the waist up, cradling her breasts. She said, "This hurts. I'd like to just chop them off."
>"Shhh," the lumberjack said. His voice was so quiet. He told her he'd read about this. He said, "You're engorged. We have to get some of the milk out."
>He brought Leslie a plastic mixing bowl full

of hot water; he brought hot washcloths. He said, "Lean into the water." He said, "Relax, as much as you can." He cupped one breast and covered it with the hot washcloth. He held her breast in the palm of his hand, and with the tips of his fingers, he pressed, firmly, gently, as jets of milk squirted into the mixing bowl. Leslie's husband said, "Go ahead and cry." The milk was cloudy in the water. Clouds of milk floated across the surface.

This is what Leslie's grief was like: her grief was pure. It said, *You can relax in me. You can trust me.* She could float down a river on it. It would cleanse her. It would feed her. She could wrap herself up in it. It would lull her to sleep.

This is what Leslie's guilt was like: her guilt was shameful and covert. She could try to run from it; she could try to outwit it. But it would find her. It would starve her. It wrapped itself around her and squeezed. It said, *If you want to remember her, you can't ever forget about me.*

Roses from the gas station. Fudge brownies from the bakery. Boxes of chocolate, bath oils, magazines from the drugstore. Leslie's husband brought her many gifts. One day, on his way home from the woods, he stopped at the drugstore and

Windows and Words

bought a coloring book of farm animals and a box of crayons. He said, "I'm running out of ideas."

Side by side, Leslie and her husband sat, coloring. She colored a cat gray; he colored a dog brown. There was something soothing about this, something comforting about watching a pale page fill with color. She pressed the crayon hard around the outline of a chicken and colored the inside yellow, lightly, with even strokes.

One picture after another, Leslie and her husband colored.

They played board games – Scrabble, Monopoly, Battleship.

They played cards – Blackjack, Rummy, War.

While her husband was in the woods, Leslie played Solitaire, one hand after another.

Sometimes, she cheated.

There was a morning when Leslie woke up and found a shock of deep purple blood in the crotch of her underwear. It turned redder and brighter as the day wore on. Of course, there weren't any tampons in the house. It pissed her off that her body could do this without her permission.

Many things pissed her off, including these:

Aunt Lois, who said, "It was God's will."

Her father-in-law, who said, "What you kids need to do is get busy and make another baby."

Her mother, who told her to take a hot

shower and go for a long walk. "And get on the Pill."

Her husband, who wanted to make love.

When he hooked his leg over hers in bed one night, murmuring something about danger and play, Leslie told him to leave her alone.

Leslie refused to make love to her husband, yet she had sex with the man who pumped out their septic system.

Why did she do this?

Was it the sex?

It was. The sex meant everything. Leslie now believed that sex and love were separate. She found she preferred the memory of sex to the actual thing. Her memory idealized it in a way her body couldn't. Her body remembered being touched, but her mind couldn't remember what he looked like. Her mind distilled what her body remembered, and later, alone, touching herself, she felt terribly lonely.

Acting on desire, Leslie thought, is just another way to avoid yourself.

She still dreamed about the wicked whore of Babylon. The whore paraded through town on horseback, laughing and peeking in windows, same as always. Only this time, in this dream, the whore was Leslie.

One night, Leslie and her husband were in

the living room: he was watching television; she was looking out the window. It was dark outside, and all she could see was a reflection of herself. Every time a commercial came on, her husband glanced over at her and said, "I love you."

The first time he said it, Leslie didn't answer.
The second time, she said, "I know."
The third time, she said, "I love you, too."
She knew these were the worst words she could say, but she said them anyway. She couldn't think of what she should say; it was too complicated to repair everything that had happened, so she opted for the easier phrase.

It was a way of filling in the silence.

It was a silence she wouldn't be able to fill the next day when the septic system man returned. He traced the marks on her stomach – gently, curiously – and he said, "You've had a baby."

Leslie pressed his hand against her flat stomach. She pushed his hand between her legs. She closed her eyes. The septic system man had a moustache and a crew cut. His hair between her fingers smelled like shampoo; his skin smelled like powder. He told Leslie he thought she was pretty. He said he had a wife he cared about very much. He said it was important Leslie know that up front.

Leslie said, "Please don't talk."

The septic system man liked Leslie. He found her needy and vulnerable and sweet.

He would mistake this for love.

Approximate to Salvation

This is what amuses my father:

The cigarette he put in the dog's mouth.

The sight of himself with two balloons under his shirt.

One of his children asking, "Where's Mom," and his reply: "She went out to take a shit and the hogs ate her."

Candy, the woman wearing fringed dresses in beach party movies, who can make things fall just by shaking.

It always begins with falling.

Falling, and my father telling me, *I am going to save you from yourself.* It begins when I am three years old, and I have fallen from my upstairs bedroom window because I was pushing too hard against the screen. Twenty-seven pounds that is me falls, window to ground, and nothing is broken, nothing is bleeding, which is how my mother determines how significant an injury is – *If you're not hemorrhaging, you're okay* – and my mother who has been gathering eggs drops her basket, and my father who has been fiddling with the tractor engine drops his wrench, and only then do I begin to cry. He whisks me away, and in the kitchen is the wooden paddle that's kept under the sink with the dish soap and the window cleaner and the bleach. *You could have died*, he says. He says, *I'm going to save you from what you might do to yourself.* He hits so hard that I piss on the linoleum. My mother stands in the doorway, waiting, but not watching, and after he throws the paddle across the room, disgusted, she says, *You sure gave Daddy a scare.* She says, *Let's clean this mess up.*

I have a teddy bear. It's three feet high – bigger than me. My teddy bear is a boy; all teddy bears are boys, and my name is Kristin, and my bear's name is Chris. Chris has two arms that jut out, and I move into them. His stiff arms rest against my shoulders. He holds me. Then I am on top of him, my cheek pressed against his. I straddle him, rubbing between-my-legs against his plump stomach. It feels good, but then it feels bad, and I punch him in the guts until I feel better.

I'm going to save you from yourself.

He says it again when I am five, holding out my hand for a stray dog to lick. *He'll bite you, you know, just like this.* When I am nine, and pissing on the floor again because I dropped an ice cube on the floor, and instead of throwing it in the sink, I put it in his iced tea. *See this garbage? This is where your supper is coming from.* When I am twelve, and seen talking to an unknown man in a car. *He could've grabbed you and locked you in his trunk, just like this.* When I am fifteen, and growing a zit farm on my chin. *This is how you wash your face.* When I am seventeen, and in danger of flunking Home Economics. He stands me in front of a skillet, and every egg yolk that breaks is another one I have to eat.

Why do you do these things? Your brothers do what they're supposed to do; why can't you?

I don't know.

I don't know. Are you dumb? Is that why you don't know?

No.

Why, then?

I don't know.

How could you not know?

I must be a dummy?

Wrong answer. I'm in trouble again: for having a smart mouth or for admitting to stupidity. Take your pick, but I'm not going to win.

Here is what angers my father:

Lies, lying, and liars.

Pork chops that have been frozen.

A newspaper someone else has read.

Sickness: coughing, sneezing, puking, fevers.

When I am eleven years old, I believe that my father is bigger than God, but definitely not as quiet. He is everywhere. He sees everything. He knows even more. The last time my mother and brothers and I bow our heads to pray is the time my father revises our prayer: *Daddy is good. Daddy is great. Thank Daddy for this food. Amen.*

My mother says, "Gordon, that's uncalled

for."

My father says, "Oh, it's called for all right. I called for it."

My brother, who has recently been converted by another seven-year-old, is upset. "I want to say it the right way!" he says. "I don't want Jesus to be mad at me!"

"He won't be," my mother assures him. "He knows it's not your fault."

"It's not my fault if Jesus is mad at him," says my father. "Is it, Kristin?"

"Nope," I cheerfully agree. These moments when my father wants me on his side are rare, but whenever they do occur, I'm more than happy to oblige. Besides, I've been enlightened because before I thought "God is good" was all one word, Latin or something.

My youngest brother stops eating to ask for more. He's just five, and the only one of us who hasn't been baptized – something my father takes great delight in. *Barabbus*, my father calls him. *My little heathen.* At this time, my youngest brother is my father's favorite child. Not only does he look like the old man – blue eyes, black hair, beaky nose – but he also acts like him, stubborn and unrelenting. Even at five, my youngest brother cannot be proven wrong.

This will change as my brothers get older; my middle brother will become my father's favorite child. He will become the star of the family, the example my father will point to, again and again, evidence of how he can indeed raise a good kid. My middle brother looks nothing like the old man; he is slim and tall, blond like my mother. He is quiet and well-mannered. Soft-spoken. Hard-working. His blue eyes don't give dirty looks. He does what he is supposed to do when he is supposed to do it. He is who my father thinks he would have been had he been given the chance.

My brothers are not punished as I am punished. They are not hit or grounded or made to kneel on hard kernels of popcorn. The only action my father takes against them is something I am spared from simply because I am a girl: it happens when my brothers have been caught rough housing.

My father has them push the coffee table against the wall, the television into a corner. *You boys want to carry on? Then carry on. And do it right.* They must now move rough housing into real fighting. My brothers, eleven and nine years old, fourteen and twelve, seventeen and fifteen, circle each other warily. My father eggs them on:

What are you, girls? The loser has to put on one of Kristin's dresses.

Are you waiting for your nail polish to dry? Worried you'll mess up your pretty hair-do? Get mad!

One of them throws a half-hearted punch. They aren't mad at each other; they're just boys with too much energy. The other one hits back, a nice, easy punch. Then my father reminds one of how the other broke his bow. Or how one got the other into trouble three years ago.

Approximate to Salvation

Remember that? my father says. *How could you forget about that?* One grabs the other by the neck and wrestles him to the floor. They flip like fish. They hurt each other. They say, *I hate you, motherfucker.* They say, *Fuck you, motherfucker.* They say, *Suck my dick, motherfucker.*

My father is referee, coach to both sides, spectator. He gives breaks between rounds. *Ding! Ding!* He penalizes for dirty fighting. These are the rules: no hair pulling, no biting, no crying – that's how girls fight. No grabbing anybody's balls – that's how sissies fight. Should someone break a rule, he must stand solid while the other hits however and wherever he pleases.

My mother says, "Enough, Gordon, I mean it."

My father says, "It's enough when I say it's enough. It hasn't been enough yet."

When the fight ends, he chooses the winner. Both boys are sobbing. My father holds up the winner's arm and pronounces him the heavyweight champion of the world. His thumb becomes a microphone: "Mr. Henderson, you are the heavyweight champion of the world. How does it feel?" The champion must help the loser from the floor. They must then shake hands. Then they have to go to the bedroom they share and get ready for bed.

There is a lesson in all of this, my father says. This will teach the boys how to fight. They will be able to help each other. By breaking each other down, they will emerge closer to each other. *You gotta respect a guy who can beat the shit out of you.* He says he is showing the boys how to be men. This is what he says he is teaching them:

Don't hit a man from behind.

Don't hit a woman, not even when she is asking for it.

Chew on the lining of your cheek and you won't cry.

This is what they eventually learn:

Don't rough house when the old man's around.

I'll tell you what my father does to be nice:

Extravagant gifts for good causes – any charity or fund raiser that has to do with kids.

Easter seals, church car washes, candy sales, raffle tickets.

Any kid who needs to be saved – money for them to buy cigarettes, money for them to buy milk, diapers, winter coats.

My father tries to help a girl he sees walking up and down the street in front of his car wash at night. He owns five car washes, and this one is in a bad neighborhood, a neighborhood full of dirt bags, and he wants to save this girl from becoming one. He stops her from leaning into a car. She is several years older than me, around sixteen, skinny and pretty. Her name is Sabrina. She already has a child, and my father brings both Sabrina and her baby home for supper one night. This is not something that my mother is prepared for, but she smiles and admires the baby and sets an extra plate.

We don't eat with Sabrina again after that,

but she calls our house. She says, "Mrs. Henderson, is Gordon there?" She says, "Can I talk to your daddy?" My father takes her calls in another room. He says, "She's just a kid. She's all alone. She doesn't have anyone else." He says, "She needs my help."

Then there are middle-of-the-night phone calls that disconnect when my mother answers. Hang-up calls early in the morning. Hang-up calls during supper. My mother gets our number changed, but the hang-up calls continue.

There is a call one night after supper. It's Sabrina. My mother tells her that Mr. Henderson is sleeping, and no, she will not wake him, and don't call here again. Later, Sabrina shows up on our front porch. My mother meets her at the door, but doesn't let her in. "When I said don't call here, I should have included don't come here, either," my mother says. "Mr. Henderson is sleeping."

"I'm pregnant," Sabrina says, "and you know what that means."

"No," says my mother, "I must be slow. I'm afraid I don't have any idea what that means."

"It means I'm going to be living in this house."

"I don't think so," says my mother. "I think you'd better go now because I know how to make phone calls, too. I know the number for the police and I know a number to call where they take babies away from little girls and put little girls into foster homes." She closes the door, gently, quietly, so as not to wake my father who is snoring on the couch.

"You didn't see this," my mother tells me. "It never happened."

"Did any of it happen?"

"None of it."

The summer I turn thirteen I am walking down the street carrying two dollar bills and a note from my father that permits me to buy his Camels, when a tall boy in grey gym shorts and a white tee-shirt falls into step beside me. He asks me my name, and when I don't answer, he tells me his, then informs me that his family just moved here, that he plays basketball, and that he'll be a junior when school starts, and would I like to go to the movies or maybe play putt putt golf sometime? "I'm just a kid," I tell him, flatly. "I'm going into eighth grade." And because the boy blushes but does not say anything, I add, "Sorry."

It's true: I look older than I am. I have *developed*. I have *matured*. I am thirteen years old, and I have a pink bedroom, and I have dolls on my bookshelves and posters of movie stars pinned to the wall, and a dressing table with a gilded mirror and drawers full of toiletries: lipstick and eye shadow and hair spray and powder and mascara. *Toiletries* – such a strange word for the things women use to make themselves pretty.

I have every stuffed animal that anyone has ever given me. I still have Chris, my teddy bear. He has held me, and I have hugged him and punched him and rocked my body against his. I think of the boy in the grey gym shorts. He has kidnapped me and taken me away. He forces himself on me. He makes me do things and makes me tell him that I like it. Like when I'm walking down the street and men in cars honk at me. Like when I walk past men and hear them whistle at me. They say, *Wish I had a porch to go with that swing. Wish I had some milk to go with that shake.* I take all of this as a compliment; I'm so flattered.

Chris is pear-shaped now; his stuffing has shifted. He is patched: in a rage, I pierce his back with a pair of scissors, and he hemorrhages. His stuffing leaks, but my mother stitches him back up for me.

There is a little boy I babysit; he is four years old and his name is Phillip. His mother is a friend of my mother's, and she drops him off at our house while she's running errands. He's so cute, this Phillip; he's got brown eyes and that dorky little boy haircut. His stomach sticks out. His lip pops out when he's mad at me. But he's rarely mad at me. He loves me. He says, *This is a surprised face*, and he opens his eyes and his mouth very wide. *This is an angry face*, and he scowls. *This is a sad face*, and he frowns. *This is a happy face*, and he smiles and holds out his arms for me to pick him up. *Show me your faces*, he says, and I do the best I can.

Phillip is in my pink bedroom with me. My mother is in the kitchen, washing dishes and talking on the telephone. I hear her say, "She was in labor for *how* long?" I let Phillip play with my stuffed animals; I show him my toiletries. *Pretend you're a baby*, I suggest, and he falls limp to the floor, on his back, gently waving his arms, gently kicking his feet. *Ga ga*, he says.

You're a wonderful baby, I tell him. *Such a purdy widdle baby.*

Mama, he says. *Mama.*

Does Baby have a dirty diaper? I say, and he nods his head. *Does Baby want his mama to change his diaper?* and he nods.

I slide down his pants; I pull down his underwear. His penis shrivels in the cold. *I'm a widdle baby*, he says.

You're a very cute baby, I tell him. I sprinkle talcum powder on him; when I flip him over and sprinkle powder on his butt, I can't help rubbing it. His butt is so little, smooth. *I love you, Phillip,* I tell him. *You know that?*

He nods.

But what if I was mean to you? What would you do then?

I would be sad, he says. He says, *Are we done now?*

Sure.

We play zoo, and we play chase and hide-and-go-seek, and his mother picks him up and pays me five dollars, and as soon as they're gone, I lock myself in my bedroom, and I rock against Chris, remembering.

At fourteen, I turn serious. I leave smiling up to my mother. Prettiness, too, though my mother needs to use lipstick and eyeliner and hair spray and padded bras to make herself look real. Without them, she's as flat and pale as paper. She's not thin anymore, though. Every year that passes, she becomes another size larger.

I'm not fat, but I'm definitely fleshy. My mother once asked the doctor: *Is there too much of Kristin?* My mother once told me: *You'd better watch out. I already caught my man.*

But every day my mother bakes: chocolate chip cookies and Dutch apple pies and caramel brownies. I eat what she bakes, plus I eat candy bars and potato chips and packaged cupcakes that I buy at the gas station down the street. I hoard these things in my bottom dresser drawer and I eat them even when I'm not hungry. Even when I think one more bite might make me puke.

But I don't puke. Instead I feel powerful and big. This is a secret I have; this is some control I have. My father tells me I'm getting fat. He makes me a bet: he bets me a hundred dollars that I will weigh 175 pounds before I turn twenty-five. He tells me I'm going to lose. He tells me to start saving my money.

My mother cooks. My brothers and I never eat cold cereal for breakfast. We come home from school at lunchtime and there is a hot lunch waiting for us. Suppers are a holy trinity: meat, potato, vegetable. I hear about sugary cereals and baloney sandwiches and tuna fish casseroles from friends at school, and though I have never eaten such meals, I crave them. But I eat steak. All the time, my family is having steak for supper. Or leg of lamb. Or ham and turkey, even in the middle of summer. I eat so much steak that I resent cows.

But I don't realize that this is eating well. I think I come from a poor family because I hear my parents arguing about money. Because my mother clips coupons and drives from supermarket to supermarket shopping for the best deals. My mother tells me she can't afford to buy the Nikes that I so desperately need to fit in with other ninth graders. She tells me to make last year's coat do again this year even though the sleeves are too short. She patches my jeans. She cuts my hair herself.

Details of this kind of suffering I will use at a later time, even after I realize that we were not as poor as my mother was stingy. When I am attending a private college on a scholarship, these details of poverty become interesting things to say, ice breakers of sorts, because those whose parents pay full tuition and those whose parents send them to Colorado for Christmas and the Bahamas for Spring Break will think it romantic when I gleefully admit that I came from a very poor blue collar family.

But college is a long time away when you are fourteen. I can't stop myself from getting into trouble; I haven't resolved why I do the things I do. On Easter Sunday, my father catches me biting the head off of a chocolate bunny only minutes before supper. He demonstrates with a knife the proper way to eat Easter chocolate: you cut off the piece you want, then you eat it. Like a human being, not like a dog. And you don't eat chocolate before

Approximate to Salvation

sitting down to supper.

My mother has prepared a grand holiday meal: a ham studded with cloves and pineapples and maraschino cherries. Sweet potatoes and mashed potatoes (only she and I know they came from a box), and gravy, and corn, and asparagus. We eat in silence for a few minutes before my father realizes that he is not finished with me. If I'm going to eat a chocolate Easter bunny like a dog, why not eat my supper like a dog? It makes sense to him. He asks each of my brothers if it makes sense to them. They have no choice but to agree that it does. My mother points out that it doesn't make sense to her, but this observation is ignored. I am to eat my supper with my hands.

Ordinarily, this wouldn't bother me. I lick clean other people's cherry pie plates. But I know this is supposed to upset me, and I play the part. I am learning. *Just do what he asks of you*, my mother drills. *Don't try to argue with him. Be what he wants and he'll leave you alone.*

But I can't outsmart the old man. He is always one step ahead of me. Looking remorseful and crying is not enough. He wants to know where the Polaroid is. He wants my mother to take a picture of me eating mashed potatoes with my fingers, brown gravy sliding down my elbows, because he hasn't seen a dog using a napkin yet. My mother quietly tells him she doesn't know where the camera is.

"Find it," he says. "You find it."

"I might not have any film."

Of course she has film; she took pictures of us in our Easter clothes just this morning. Of course there is film in the camera; my mother never takes more than one picture at a time. "Say Easter Bunny!" my father says. He waves the picture back and forth to speed up its development, and then he hurls it at me.

"See how you look?"

I don't want to see but the picture is there, right beside my plate. The girl in the picture has a face that's blotchy and fat. There are creases across her forehead. Her eyes are squinty and small and very dark. There are clumps of food in her hair and stains on the back of her sleeve. Is this how I am? I didn't know I could be this ugly.

My father says: "See why I have to treat you this way? I'll save you yet."

My mother tells me that he loves his kids and that is why he is so hard on them. He expects a lot out of you because he believes in you. He wouldn't love you like this if he really believed you were stupid.

My mother is married to a man who has the kind of temper that sends pot roasts flying out of windows and overturns dressers and kicks in television screens. The people at Sears must have thought this family loved to watch television with all the televisions they bought. They must have thought there was a television in every room when there was only one television and it is the focal point of the

Approximate to Salvation

living room. Everything is arranged to fit around the television. My mother talks on the telephone all morning to one girlfriend, then another, and from 12:30 until 4:00, she watches soap operas. During the commercial breaks, she cleans, running the vacuum, dusting, folding laundry, washing a few dishes at a time. *Commercial cleaning*, she likes to call it, and after the sponsors have given their word, she sits perched on the couch, elbows on her knees, dust rag in her hand. This is another secret I am instructed to keep: my mother doesn't want my father to know how much television she watches.

He doesn't need to know. Look, I changed that algebra grade for you, didn't I? I got you those forty dollar jeans you had to have, didn't I? That was my coupon money, you know. I take care of you, you take care of me.

One day, I am angry with my mother. Maybe she is nagging me about cleaning up my room. Maybe she's caught me in a lie. Maybe she slaps me for being spiteful. I say, "I'm telling Daddy. I'm telling him that all you do all day is watch television."

My mother is puzzled. She says, "Why? Why would you want to bite the hand that feeds you?"

My father watches television every night after supper. *Make my couch*, he says, and my mother drapes a sheet over the couch, and I fetch his pillows and bring him his newspaper and his ashtray and a glass of iced tea. He watches the news and the stock market report, then he watches hour long shows full of action: car chases and drug busts and people shooting at each other. By 9:00, he is asleep, and if someone is brave enough to change the channel, he wakes up.

I am fifteen years old. I hear my mother talking on the telephone to one of her girlfriends. She is talking about recipes, she is talking about things she likes to eat, she is talking about dieting. I hear her say, "Yeah, a couple Ex Lax take care of that easy enough."

It is so simple that I can't believe I never thought of it before. This is my new habit: shoplifting food from the gas station, shoplifting laxatives from the drug store. You fill yourself with junk; you rid yourself of the junk. You control input and output. You lose weight. You find a body that was hidden from you before and you realize what it can do for you.

How it can save you.

My father is susceptible to pretty things. Look at his house. You'd never know that three men live in this house as pretty and clean and white as it is. Look at his daughter. Pretty and clean and white. Sixteen years old. He doesn't hit her anymore; how could you hit someone who smiles so sweetly, who raises and lowers her eyelashes, who blushes at the slightest indecency. Such a dainty girl. Such delicate manners. Napkin across her lap. She says please and thank you and may I and excuse me. She serves him from the left and clears his plate from the right. He yells at her because he must; it has always been in his nature to yell. He punishes

Approximate to Salvation

her because he must; she is still a liar and a sneak because she has always been a liar and a sneak. The body has changed, but not the girl in the body.

Or has she?

She stands on her tiptoes to kiss his cheek before bed at night. Once, she kisses his neck and sucks a bit of skin. She empties his ashtray before it's full; she brings him aspirin and glasses of iced tea before he knows he has a headache, before he knows he's thirsty. She picks lint off his shirts. She tells him he needs a haircut; she likes his new beard. His stomach isn't fat, she says, it's cute. She's there at the door to greet him when he comes home from work. "Hi, Daddy," she says. "How was your day?" Her voice is girlish, but full of womanly concern. If she were a dog, she'd roll over and show her belly. She can see this confuses him. She likes his discomfort. She imagines him wondering: Is she flirting with me?

Her clothes aren't provocative, but the way she wears them is. His rule is that skirts can be no shorter than the length of her arms, and he tests this rule before she leaves for school in the mornings. But her arms are short – he says they're shorter than they should be. She borrows his sweaters; they are huge on her, almost as long as her skirts. The collars slip over her shoulders, exposing white or black or red bra straps. She takes good care of his sweaters, returning them to his closet freshly laundered, but when he wears them, he will smell her perfume. When he holds them up to his body, he will imagine them on hers.

He stands behind her when she is sitting at the kitchen table doing her calculus. She looks up at him. "Yes," she says. "Do you want something?"

He opens her bedroom door without knocking and finds her in her nightgown, painting her toenails. "Yes?" she says. "Can I do something for you?"

Much later, she will discover that he puts aside money for her at a bank other than the one where his wife banks. He is putting aside money for when she graduates from high school. There is a little restaurant on the south side of town that has been out of business for years. He plans to buy it and present it to her – that way, she won't need to leave home and go to college. She can live right here in his house and run this restaurant. He will go there for his coffee in the mornings. She can fry his eggs. He will tell the customers, "That's my girl."

On a Friday night, we are watching television and eating pizza even though we have eaten supper not three hours before. We hear fire engines scream past our house and up the street. My father throws down his crust and says, "Get me a clean shirt." I bring him one, a blue and green plaid, and he is putting on his socks when he says, "You coming, Kristin?" My mother looks up and smiles. There haven't been any major battles between my dad and me for a long time, and she takes responsibility for this. I know she's thinking, *See? I told you that if you just acted right. He'd come around.* My youngest brother looks hurt because he isn't invited and my middle brother doesn't even look up.

We get into my father's truck and we drive around for a while. "I thought we were going to the fire," I say.

"We are. No big rush."

I don't mind. This is the first time I can remember him asking me to go somewhere with him. He pulls into a convenience store and comes out with a pack of cigarettes and two candy bars. "I can't eat this," I say. "I just ate pizza."

"Oh, eat it," he says. "I bought it for you. Eat it. Open mine for me."

We drive around some more, and he fiddles with the radio, and surprises me when he knows all the words to all the songs. "Where are we going?" The candy doesn't even taste good, I'm so full. I'm feeling sick.

"Where are we going," he mimics. "What's the rush? Where's the fire?" He thinks this is very funny, and I laugh, too.

The cheese plant is on fire. The smoke is so black that you can see it against the night sky. There are crowds of people standing everywhere. We can't find a place to park, so we keep driving. He reaches over and takes my hand.

"You look better to me than your mother ever did."

Jerking away is the first thing to do; it happens before you even fully realize what he's saying. Your heart pounds. You don't think – there is nothing to think. "Oh, come on," he says.

"You know what I'm talking about. You know what you've been doing."

"No, I don't."

"Yes, you do."

You shake your head. "I don't."

"You know you do."

"I want to go home."

"Krissy – "

"*Now*, please."

He's angry. "Oh, sure. Run home and tell your mother. You two are always against me. You're always talking about me. But you don't need to tell your mother anything about this. She doesn't need to know. All it'll do is upset her."

You don't say anything.

"I'm not going to do anything to you," he says. "Not if you don't want me to. Okay?" He's driven so far out of town that it takes close to an hour to get back home. "Okay?" he says. You don't speak during this ride, except once, to tell him to pull over because you're going to throw up. When he pulls into the driveway, he says it again. "Okay?"

"How was the fire?" your mother says.

You say, "It was okay."

This is the kind of secret a girl like Kristin keeps. She reminds herself that wanting to do something and actually doing it are two separate things. She quits going to church because the church sees this differently. The church says that the thought and the action are the same sin. She keeps telling herself that the church has to be wrong.

This is the kind of secret she keeps – even from herself. She reaches a place where she won't allow herself to think about it. She's ashamed of herself for all the games she played that brought this on. She quits playing those games. She quits playing all games. She does what she is supposed to do when she is supposed to do it, the way she is supposed to do it. No more being half-assed. She studies hard because it is the only way she can think of to get herself out. She only passes Home Economics because she gets to do extra credit sewing projects – her mother gets to do extra credit sewing projects. And when she graduates, and a little restaurant on the south side of town is presented to her, she turns it down. "It's not what I want," she says.

"What do you want?" her father says. She's hurt his feelings. She doesn't know this from looking at him. She doesn't look at him at all if she can help herself. There are new rules now and she follows them. She pretends that nothing is wrong. She says thank you on Christmas morning and she kisses the air beside his cheek on Father's Day. She only knows when his feelings are hurt because her mother tells her so.

"I don't know what I want," she says. "I just know what I don't want."

The place where she begins to tell what happened is college.

But she doesn't tell it the way it really

happened.

When the subject comes up with other women, she says she, too, was raped. She makes the story interesting, of course, and big. She was walking to her car after a day of shopping at the mall and a strange man abducted her and drove her around for a while, then he raped her and left her for dead on the side of the road. Or she was raped on a date. She was out on a date with this boy, dinner and a movie, and after the movies, they were driving around, and they came to this big field that was on fire, and the boy wanted to fool around, and she didn't, so he raped her. Other women say, Oh, Kristin, I'm so sorry that happened to you. That's terrible. How awful. Kristin says, I know. She doesn't feel like a phony and a liar even though she knows she is. Eventually, she tires of telling these stories. She tires of hearing others' stories. Eventually, she tries to reach a place where she really doesn't think about it at all.

It almost saves me.

Sick Child

She'll remember this as a friendlier time: he's coughing, but only because he can't not cough. His cough is a barking seal; it's a clogged drain. It's her name in the middle of the night. As tempting as it may be to ignore him, to put a pillow over her head, to pull the comforter over her face, to close her eyes and count to ten in every language she knows – English, Japanese, Pig Latin – he'll still cough; she'll still hear him.

He's so rarely sick that she isn't sure what she's supposed to do. In a strange way, this is a good thing: he's rarely sick because of her cautious parenting – a new toothbrush every month, antibacterial hand soap, long walks in mountain air, Flintstones vitamins. Should she plug in the vaporizer? Fill the bathroom with steam? Rub him down with Vicks?

She was once like him, a child with a winter cold. She was a girl in western Pennsylvania, and her father did all of the above, plus he made her lie face down on the ironing board. He hoisted up the end her feet dangled from, while her mother held her legs down, and her brothers pounded on her back. Near her head was a stainless steel pan for her to spit the phlegm from her lungs into. This remedy worked because her father believed a cold could be bullied. *Mind over body,* he said, thus ensuring no one ever brought home bronchitis again.

Her son is sitting on the edge of his bed, a thin sheet draped around his shoulders. He's wearing only his underwear. His face is pale, his eyes are glassy. His hair is slicked back with sweat. "Where are your pajamas?" she asks.

"I got hot."

Does he have a fever?

Touching his forehead, she can't tell. She imagines the long search for the thermometer, sticking it under his tongue, his protests, the lights she'd have to turn on. "Just relax," she tells him. "Take it easy. You'll be all right, I promise." She carries him back to her bed, where she strokes his damp hair, murmuring to him, and they both fall asleep only to both wake minutes later.

He's coughing.

It's a terrible sound.

There's a bottle of children's cough syrup in the medicine cabinet, but she knows it's expired. She hasn't given him any since that night more than a year ago, the night when his father, who was then her husband, went to a funeral back in Pennsylvania, some old maid aunt dead by natural causes. This was the night her lover was coming over, and she wanted her son to go to bed early and sleep soundly. She thought mixing a spoonful of cherry-flavored cough syrup in his Pepsi would help him along. It was a trick she'd picked up from a talk show, a white trash mother accused of doing it so she could go party, and the audience hissed and booed.

But the trick backfired. Instead of making him groggy, instead of knocking him out, the cough syrup made him hyper. *Supercharged,* his grandmother would have said. *Wired for sound.* It was after midnight before she finally got him to sleep, and when her lover did come over, she was so tense and agitated, feeling so guilty – *I slipped my own kid a Mickey!* – that she just wanted to get the whole thing over with so the night could end.

Her son is still coughing; she still hears him. When will this end?

Her son is six years old, and as far as he knows, his cough could be with him always, like the scar on his elbow from the time he fell out of a tree at the park, like his mother's boyfriend, like the note Mrs. Quintera sent home saying he's a glue-eater, like the scar near the corner of his left eye from the time he doesn't know what happened. His cough could stay inside him and grow with him, getting bigger as he does. It could follow him around like the puppy he's always wanted but can't have because they live in an apartment complex, or like the maybe-someday baby brother or sister his mother occasionally pines for which is something he doesn't ever want. His cough could be his friend, his ally, his trusted servant. He coughs, and his mother listens.

His eyelids flutter and close, and when he pushes them open, he's not in his bed or his mother's. She's moved him again: now he's lying under a blanket on the couch, and the television is on, blue light in a dark night room, and his mother is stretched out on the floor beneath him, smoking a cigarette and staring at the ceiling. He disapproves of her smoking and coughs a little to let her know. But the little cough turns into a big one: it sucks all the air out of him, filling his lungs with barbed wire and brittle twigs and dusty cotton and flecks of tobacco from the bottom of his mother's purse. *You wanted to scare her*, his cough tells him. *It's your own fault.*

His mother sits up and takes his hand. She's counting in the Japanese he learned in karate class and then taught to her: *ichi, ni, san, shi, go.* "Just relax," she tells him. "Remember: mind over body."

On the day of the scar near his eye, during the ride to the hospital, his mother counted to three hundred and eighty-eight. One minute, he was at her boyfriend's house, where they'd gone to do laundry, and he was all by himself in the back yard, sent there by her boyfriend and told to play quietly. The next minute, he was in the emergency room, where a doctor with a needle that looked like a fishing hook was stitching up a small but deep hole near the corner of his left eye. *Can you tell me what happened?* the doctor said. He told her he didn't know. The doctor asked his mother to step out of the room. *Now will you tell me what happened?* the

Sick Child

doctor said, and he told her, *Something did, but I don't know what.*

His father called from Pennsylvania, and his grandfather called, and there was also Mrs. Quintera, and the check-out girl at the grocery store, and the old lady at the bank, all asking, *What happened?* All saying, *C'mon, you can tell me.* His grandfather told him that if he didn't 'fess up, then Santa Claus wouldn't come to Colorado, nor the Easter Bunny, nor the Tooth Fairy, and his mother, who'd been listening on the other extension, said, *Bullshit,* and told him to say good-bye to Grandpa. His mother's boyfriend said, *That kid knows good and well what happened; he just won't tell.* His father said, *Where was Mom?*

Right now, his father is asleep in a bed fifteen hundred miles away; his father doesn't even know that the best boy in the world can't stop coughing. Outside, a car glides across the icy parking lot. Inside, light from the television flickers, and his mother is counting. "Ichi, ni, san, shi, go," she says. "Go! Go away, you stupid cough. Get out of Carleton's body."

She sounds mad. She doesn't know his cough is something he can see when he closes his eyes. His cough looks like a thistle stuck to a sock, a burr stuck to a shoelace. It's holding a long pointy stick like a spear; it's twirling the spear like a baton. The spear is tied to a weeping willow branch with a shoelace, and his cough flicks it at him like a whip, narrowly missing his eye. His cough is saying, *Ichi, ni, san, shi, are you sure you want me to go? If you let me stay, I'll be your best friend.*

"Mom?"

"Just close your eyes. Breathe, sweetheart. I want you to relax."

His mother's voice is low and smooth. Her hands are soft. Her eyes are brown, like his. She's counting, and he's listening. He's relaxing, like she wants. She's turning up the heat; the furnace clanks and moans. Hot dry air kicks out. His breathing turns slow and shallow.

He's asleep.

But for how long?

His mother is sitting on the drafty floor, watching him. Her son is sleeping, but not peacefully. He's wheezing. He's grinding his teeth. His eyelids are fluttering, his eyeballs are rolling; he's the witness to something happening in a dream. The scar near the corner of his eye is pink, but the doctor told her it'll eventually fade, and as he grows, and his skin stretches, it will slide across his face. *My guess is he gouged himself with a sharp object*, the doctor said. His scar is a small dent, no bigger than a pencil eraser, and she runs her finger over it.

He's the only child she's ever been around, so she doesn't have any basis for comparison, but he strikes her as a strange little kid, so dreamy and unfocused, like the day she ran her fingers through his hair and found it was stiff, as if he hadn't rinsed the shampoo out of it, and when she asked him, he said, *I must've forgot.* Or like the night she went in to check on him before going to bed, and there he was, uncovered, asleep, and stripped of his pajamas,

Sick Child

with a brown teddy bear stuffed down the front of his underwear. Or like the day his teacher sent home a note saying that he'd first squirted glue on Joe's arm, was warned, and then was caught, "gleefully lapping a substantial amount of glue out of his cupped palm."

Your son is a glue-eater, said her lover in a way that, to her, seemed critical and unfriendly. She'd replied, *Maybe so. But every class needs one,* and she kept the note, smoothed out the creases and put it in her son's baby book, along with the strands from his first haircut and the hospital discharge papers from the day he got his stitches. That day had been almost a month ago, and still, her son's father won't let it go, asking, *Where were you? He could have lost an eye. You don't even know what happened. Why weren't you watching him?*

"I was in the basement," is what she tells her son. "You got hurt during the rinse cycle, and I was adding fabric softener. Or maybe it happened when I was sitting on the couch, kissing and being kissed." She runs her finger across her son's brow, then kisses his scar. "I don't remember," she says.

Her lover is in his fifties; he's never been married, and he is not a lover of children. In a strange way, this is a good thing: it protects her from her whims, from the stirring she feels when confronted with the babies she sees in department stores and on television and in her own mind. Her lover pays for her birth control, reminding her that it's important to take her pill at the same time every day, thus ensuring there are no accidents. *Happy or otherwise*, he says. *I don't want anyone else. I only want you*, and this, too, is good. It protects her from the jealousy she felt last June, when her son and his father were together, and her son seemed to forget about her, hugging his father at the Pittsburgh airport, not returning her wink, not holding her hand, his father needing to remind him, *Say good-bye to Mom. Tell her you'll see her in three months*, before she boarded her flight back to Denver. It's the same jealousy she'd felt only moments after her son was born, and her husband left her lying there on the table, alone, sweaty and exhausted; he stood with his back to her, cradling the baby in his arms. By July, she missed her son terribly, much more than she'd anticipated, and her lover said, *It's really good with just you and me.*

I can't be with that kid every second of the day, she'd told his father. *He's fine. He didn't lose his eye. Isn't that what's important? Does it really matter how it happened?*

Her son's father said, *You tell me.*

Outside, snow is still falling. She gets up and looks out the window to where her neighbors, a college girl and her boyfriend, are drunkenly coasting across the icy parking lot on plastic lunch trays, the boyfriend giving the girl a hard push, the girl on the tray, sliding, spinning to a stop.

Inside, the apartment is unbearably hot; the living room is shrinking. It's the dry heat, the noise from the television. It's the flickering light, the blankets heaped on the floor, her sock wet from the

Sick Child

glass of water she tripped over. Her face feels greasy; her mouth tastes sticky; she needs to brush her teeth. It's her son, who is awake, filling the room with his croupy cough.

Why is he sick?

Her son doesn't know. His cough says, *You know good and well*, and the spear attached to the whip flicks at him like the forked tongue of an angry snake.

"Mom?" he says.

His mother doesn't say anything. She's pulling the curtain back over the window; she's changing the channel on the television. She hits the mute button. His mother is yawning, propping another pillow behind his head, then she's turning on the fan over the stove and lighting another cigarette. She sucks smokes in and blows it out. Smoke comes out of her nose and floats around her face.

He misses his dad.

They are two guys who can do whatever they want, like eat popcorn for supper, throw popcorn at each other, and go to movies rated P.G., like the one about the ninja warrior who had a powerful and deadly spear. *You probably won't want to tell Mom about that one*, his father said. They can go to bed wearing sweatpants instead of pajamas, and then wear those same sweatpants the next day, and not just around the house. They can wear them in public, which is something his mother won't let him do because her boyfriend thinks it's white trashy. She called him every day over the summer, her voice tiny and far away, and she told him how much she missed him, how she couldn't wait until he was home with her again, *I don't know what to do without you,* she said, but right now, she's back at the window, staring outside at something he can't see.

"Mo-om!" he says.

He coughs, and it feels like the claws of a thousand alley cats scratching against his throat. *Meow,* says his cough. *You can't have a cat because your mother is allergic to them.* But his grandparents have one, and he petted it over the summer, while his dad sat at the kitchen table talking to them about his mother; they asked him if his mother and her boyfriend ever sent him to his room, or outside, or if they ever turned on cartoons for him to watch so they could take a nap together. *Is her boyfriend mean to you? Is her boyfriend mean to her? Does he ever spend the night? How often does he come over?*

I don't know, he told them. *I can't remember.*

"Mom?" he says.

She doesn't answer.

Ichi, ni, san, she's forgotten about you, his cough says.

You can always come live with me, his father said. *Say the word, and I'll come get you. Think of the fun we'd have.*

His cough says, *Would you really leave your mother? What would she do without you?*

His cough makes him gasp for air. His face is turning red. He's coughing from deep in his lungs; he's hacking, like his lungs are crumbling, and he can't catch his breath. He can't control this or stop it from happening. His body twists, then he's falling off the couch, then his mother snatches him up, and as if by accident, they're outside in the parking lot. He's wearing Spider Man underwear; his mother is wearing a long tee-shirt, and snow flakes melt in their hair.

"Nice night," says a guy with ski goggles around his neck and a bottle of beer in his hand.

"Are you okay?" says a girl sitting on a plastic lunch tray.

"He's sick," his mother says, and she's out of breath herself. "He can't stop coughing."

But he's not coughing.

For now.

How will this end?

His mother thinks it's bound to end badly. Her son is in no shape to go to school in the morning, which means she won't be able to go to work, and her boss, a childless woman, won't be happy with her. He'll sleep most of the day, and by the day after tomorrow, he'll be feeling a bit better, but still not well enough to go to school.

That day won't be a friendly one.

On that day, he'll cough, not because he can't help it, but because she'll be ignoring him. She'll want him to get well, not because he's her son, and she loves him, which is true enough, but because she'll be sick of his sickness. She'll be sick of holding his hand and talking to him in a low smooth voice. She'll get sick of reading him books and watching his videos, of bringing him bowls of chicken noodle soup and glasses of ginger ale. She can already see limp noodles spilled and drying on the kitchen floor, dishes piling up, beds unmade, milk passing its expiration date. She can already hear her mother's voice on the telephone, *Well, dear, if you hadn't decided to remain clear across the country*; and her father's, *Make him get up and walk around. Tell him to shake it off. You baby that kid*; and her lover's, *Is he still contagious?*; and her ex-husband's, *How'd he even get sick?* She can already feel the itch in her throat and the ache in her lungs.

Outside, clouds drift across the moon.

Inside, she says, "Carleton, I can make you a cup of tea. That might help you feel better. Would you like that?"

He nods.

Once, mother and son were at the bank, in line at the drive-through window. He was sitting behind her, strapped in a car seat, when he burped, loud and wet, then he puked up pancakes and apple juice. He wasn't quite two years old that day, and he didn't seem sick – just surprised.

She quickly ran through her options: should she hurry up and rush him home, or could she go ahead and make her deposit? There was the rising stink of maple syrup, the beige streaks on his cheeks, and there was also the likelihood of checks bouncing if she didn't immediately get the money in her account.

A car pulled up behind them, and her decision was made.

Sick Child

She spoke to him in a low smooth voice – the same voice her mother had used on her father during the layoffs at Rockwell, the one she'd used on her son's father, who was then only her boyfriend, when she told him she'd missed her period. *It's okay. Everything will be all right.*

He emitted another damp belch, then he turned his face from her. He hiccupped, he was frowning, he was trembling. She knew he wanted to cry, and if he did, it would be explosive, loud and wet. It would fill the car.

Relax, baby, she said. *You'll be okay, I promise.*

He wouldn't look at her. Instead, he looked out the window. As she soothed him, he continued to stare sadly out the window, and in his profile – his forehead wrinkled, his brow furrowed, his bottom lip quivering – she could see what he'd become, how he'd be when he was a man with troubles beyond his control.

Expatriates

It was Ascension Day, a spring holiday for the Amish Dutch; they gathered their fishing poles and their tackle, and in buggies and on foot, they set out for Neshannock Creek. That's what Valentine Byler was supposed to be doing: wading into the water and casting out a line. Instead, he was in the Cappabiancos' living room with a yellow towel draped around his shoulders. It was two o'clock. Carly Cappabianco and I were spritzing Valentine's head with water from a plastic spray bottle. We were sneaking slugs of Mr. Cappabianco's beer when he wasn't looking. Kidnapping Valentine is what we were doing. But first, we had to give him a haircut.

Carly had been wanting to kidnap Valentine for years, ever since he finished his schooling and went to work in her father's pallet shop. She wants to be a teacher so she was always showing Valentine pictures of educational things: pictures of astronauts tiptoeing across the moon, pictures of pygmies frolicking in Africa. In a few hours, Carly and Mr.

Cappabianco would take Valentine to the Greyhound station in Pittsburgh, where he'd board the bus heading west, to Colorado. Right now, Carly was showing Valentine a postcard of Red Rock. There were dinosaur tracks pressed into the side of some mountain, and Valentine, utterly innocent, said, "I didn't know they had dinosaurs out there."

Carly threw her hands in the air. "That's *exactly* what I mean," she said. "There's a *perfect* example of what I've been talking about." She's very dramatic. She's Italian, of course, which is rare and exotic in New Wilmington. It was just Carly and her father, Mr. Chick Cappabianco. Her parents were in transition, trying to decide if they were going to stay married or not. Carly's mother and her little brother R. T. were spending the summer with relatives in West Virginia.

"Those Dutchmen are like a cult!" Carly was saying. "They only tell him what they want him to know. They want to keep him stupid so he can't ever leave." She got this keeping-you-stupid stuff from her father. Mr. Cappabianco accused everybody of trying to keep you stupid. The government. The media. Educators. The Pope. You don't want to sit around the table after supper with him for very long, trust me. Very depressing. He wasn't paying attention to Carly during this: the television was on, and both he and Valentine were watching it. Every so often, Mr. Cappabianco took off his baseball cap to scratch his head, then put it back on again.

Carly said, "There's a big world outside New

Wilmington, Pennsylvania, Valentine." She was shaking the postcard for emphasis. "A great big world that you don't know anything about. Do you know that?"

Valentine said, "What would I know? I'm just a dumb Dutchman."

Carly said, "I suppose you're going to find out."

Valentine said, "I suppose."

He could be like that. Sarcastic. Valentine had gone up to the eighth grade at the Amish school where he'd been taught by an Amish girl who'd gone only as far as the eighth grade, and who'd been taught by a similarly educated Amish girl, and so on. Now just suppose that Valentine's teacher's teacher didn't know dinosaurs had ever existed, let alone that they're now extinct. It's possible, you know. I think it would even be sort of nice. Comforting. You wouldn't have to wonder why dinosaurs aren't mentioned in the Bible.

Before I go on, I should tell you who I am. I'm Susan Hoyt from New Wilmington, which is a very small town in western Pennsylvania. I still answer to Sookey, my childhood nickname, but only out of habit, and I'm trying to stop. I'm an only child and I'm a cheerleader. Daddy is an accountant; my mother plays the flute. Mr. Cappabianco referred to us as White-heads. I never took it personally – he referred to everyone in New Wilmington as a Whitehead. New Wilmington is Whiteheadsville. He said if the school cafeteria was going to serve beef-a-roni on Italian Day, and macho

Expatriates

nachos on Mexican Day, then there should be a Whitehead Day where they serve grilled cheese and tomato soup. I think he's absolutely right.

When the Cappabiancos bought the house next door, Carly and I were both nine years old. Carly was a Catholic, and Catholicism fascinated me. Especially the act of Confession. I'd always longed to Confess. There's never been a child with a conscience as guilty as mine. Carly and I had this game we used to play: World Religions. I pretended to be a Catholic. Perched on the edge of the toilet seat, I confessed to Carly, the priest on the other side of the shower curtain.

Carly pretended to be a born-again Christian, influenced, no doubt, by the preachers' kids we met every August when New Wilmington hosted the Christian Missionary Alliance conference. She had me tie her to a tree in her backyard, then prepare a kettle for boiling. As I danced around her, hooting and hollering, she'd spout off Bible verses. She knew a lot of them. She even won the Vacation Bible School verse contest: the prize was a bank shaped like a globe with little brown crosses on all the countries sporting Alliance missionaries. Long ago, one of the confessions I'd made was how much I coveted that bank, and Carly gave it to me.

But there in the Cappabiancos' living room, I was already feeling guilty about what we were up to. Kidnapping Valentine. Though I'm not sure *kidnap* is the right word – Valentine was almost eighteen years old, and we did have his full cooperation. He came to the Cappabiancos, and he told them, "I'm outta here!" He was furious. His father had searched his buggy and found a boom box and a little battery-operated television, and a solar-powered calculator and a digital watch. Andy R. Byler made Valentine build a big fire, and he made Valentine throw all his stuff in that fire, and he made Valentine watch it burn.

On Ascension Day morning, Valentine abandoned his buggy in the woods and fastened his horse to a tree behind the Apple Empire. He left a note in his buggy: *So long all you shithead Dutchmens,* it said. *I'm going to Alaska.*

"Why Alaska?" we asked him.

He said, "It sounds so far away."

But I know that Valentine's mother and father say kidnapping is exactly what we did. That's what they told Sheriff Tim Chamberlain: *Those people kidnapped our son.* They still blame us — Carly and Mr. Cappabianco and me, but mostly Carly and Mr. Cappabianco — when really, all we did was *enable* Valentine to do what's known around here as jumping the fence.

At least, that's what I keep telling myself.

You see, I'm the one who cut this hair.

I'm also the one with the guilty conscience who answered the Cappabiancos' telephone.

"I'm not even sure he needs a haircut," I said. I was inching my fingers through Valentine's hair, which was thick and blond and straight: bangs level with his eyebrows, part severely down the middle, sides and back flipping up just below his ears. "He's got some split ends," I said. "He needs some conditioner, maybe. But give him a hair dryer and a dab of gel and he'll look fine."

"He'd look like a girl," Mr. Cappabianco said. Missing R. T. made him very partial to Valentine. Mr. Cappabianco often said that Valentine was the best damn worker he ever had. Once a week, he told his other Dutchmen employees that he and Valentine were running a load of pallets to Universal Rundal when really the two of them spent the afternoon on the couch, drinking Iron City Light and watching cowboy movies. They didn't talk, not even during the commercials. Mr. Cappabianco was so tickled by how much Valentine enjoyed television that he bought him a little battery-operated one, which Valentine kept hidden under the seat in his buggy. But don't get the wrong idea as others have: Mr. Cappabianco's no pervert or anything. He just got a big kick out of introducing someone to the twentieth century. He said it reminded him of Carly, as an infant, discovering she had fingers and toes.

"Cut that boy's hair," he said. "Cut his hair short."

"I don't look like any damn girl," said Valentine.

"We have to cut it, Sookey," Carly said. "If we don't, everyone will know he's a Dutchman."

"I don't know about that," I said. "Lots of guys wear their hair long. It's very in."

87

"Cut it," said Mr. Cappabianco.

"It's necessary, Sookey," said Carly.

"He won't be able to change his mind," I told them. "Once we cut it, there's no going back."

Valentine was smoking one of Mr. Cappabianco's cigarettes. Lucky Strikes, unfiltered. "I'm not going to change my mind," he said.

"He knows what he's doing, Sookey."

"Cut it," Valentine said.

Carly was holding out her hand. "Give me those scissors," she said. "I'll cut it."

"No," I said. "I will. If he's sure that's what he wants."

Valentine said, "Cut it." Cigarette smoke filtered out of his nose and curled in the air around his head.

I've lived in New Wilmington, Pennsylvania my whole life, and not a day's gone by that I haven't heard the clip clop of horses pulling Amish buggies past my house, haven't stepped over the road apples their horses leave in the street, but I never knew a Dutchman before Valentine. My mother has a hand-stitched Amish quilt that hangs over a wooden rack in our living room. It's a gorgeous quilt: little diamonds and squares of blue and gray, and in the upper left hand corner, there's a tiny snippet of red. It's beautiful. But it's not to sleep under. My mother paid over nine hundred dollars for it.

So I knew *of* the Amish. I knew *about* them. Things I learned in Social Studies, and a lot of that

Expatriates

wasn't even accurate. Like their blue front doors. I was taught the Amish Dutch paint their front doors blue when there's a daughter in the house eligible for marriage. Not so. Valentine told me. And when I asked him, well, then why the blue front doors, he'd said, "I don't know. Just because." His front door is blue, and he doesn't even have any sisters. He's the youngest of five sons. He couldn't get over that not only did we study the Amish Dutch in school, but also that one of the things we learned about them was why they have blue front doors. "And *you* think they're keeping *me* stupid," he said.

What I thought was really appalling about the Amish Dutch happened on payday at the pallet shop. Instead of writing Valentine's name across the check, Mr. Cappabianco had to make it out to Andy R. Byler, Valentine's father. That wasn't just the case for Valentine, either: this happens to all Amish boys. They don't get to keep their own pay until they're married. It's an Amish rule.

There are lots and lots of Amish rules. For instance, Dutchmen can't smoke cigarettes. They can smoke pipes, yes, and they can smoke cigars – most of them seem to enjoy Swisher Sweets. They just aren't allowed to smoke cigarettes. This doesn't seem to make a lot of sense: after all, tobacco in any form is still tobacco. But when you get right down to it, it's that tobacco-is-tobacco logic that makes me say: what difference does it make? Big deal that you can't smoke a cigarette. Smoke a cigar instead! So I wasn't going to pressure Valentine. I wasn't going to tell him he had to cut his hair. I left it up to him. It was his choice.

However.

I was not about to let Carly be the one to cut his hair. You should see what she does to her own hair. Heavy on the Aqua Net. I heard girls at school make cracks about Carly's hair. How big it was. Waterproof. It does make her stand out, look taller than she actually is. But Carly doesn't care. She's brave that way. When she was standing there, expecting me to hand over the scissors, I was thinking: *You aren't the only interesting person in this room. You aren't the only one who can make things happen.*

I was jealous of Carly. I know that. I can admit it.

Mr. Cappabianco got out his road atlas and opened it to the state of Colorado. He especially liked the areas on the map that weren't dense with little red population dots. "It's nice out west, Valentine," he was saying. "I've never been any further west than Ohio, but Tommy Crivelli tells me it's really nice out there." Tommy Crivelli was a childhood buddy of Mr. Cappabianco's who'd be picking Valentine up at the Greyhound station in Denver. "You're going to like it there. Good hunting, good fishing. Big mountains. I've always wanted to go to Colorado."

"Hold still," I said. I was working the scissors on Valentine's hair. It wasn't as easy as I'd thought it would be: his hair had never been cut in layers so I didn't have anything to follow. I was cutting blindly.

"Do you know what you're doing?" Valentine said. Hunks of hair were falling to his lap.

"Just sit still."

"Imagine, Valentine," Carly was saying. "Someone day you'll come back to New Wilmington, and you can be like one of those little old ladies from Pittsburgh and take one of those bus tours through Amish country. You can buy apple butter and a Dutch rocker! Won't that be nice?"

"Ha!" said Valentine. "I'm never coming back."

"Oh, don't give me that," said Mr. Cappabianco. "You'll be back. You have family here. You'll want to come back and see them."

"He'll be excommunicated," said Carly. "It's just like the Catholics. He'll be dead to them."

"No," Valentine said, "they'll take me back. I haven't joined our church yet. You don't join until you're eighteen. As long as I haven't joined the Church, I can leave and come back."

"Don't ever join," I told him. "That can be your safety net." I brushed the hair out of his ears and off my wrists. "There," I said. "All done."

We stood back and looked at him. You could see what big pink ears Valentine had. His scrawny neck. His whole head looked bigger, floating above his shoulders like a helium balloon.

"Not bad," said Carly.

"He's got a little bald spot," I admitted, "but

a hat'll take care of that."

"I'm not putting on that Dutchman hat ever again," said Valentine, rubbing his head. "I'll wear a ball cap. Or a cowboy hat."

"I like it," said Carly. "He looks good."

"He looks so different," I said. "Like a person not wearing their glasses." It was true. He looked startled. Blinking.

"He looks," said Mr. Cappabianco, "like the woman I saw and thought was your mother. She was driving a stick shift, and I thought, Who taught Charlotte how to drive a stick shift? But it wasn't her." Mr. Cappabianco shook his head, sadly. "That's what he reminds me of."

Valentine was slapping the hair off his shoulders and chest. "I got hair down my back," he said. "It itches like hell."

"You'll have to change your clothes," said Carly. "I can get something of R. T.'s for you to wear."

She went into R. T.'s bedroom and came out with a pile of clothes. Valentine went in R. T.'s bedroom and put them on. When we saw him again, gone were the dark blue trousers, fly fastened by hooks and eyes. Gone was the white shirt. Gone were the brown shit-kicker boots. Valentine was wearing a pair of ratty tennis shoes, patched and faded blue jeans, and a yellow tee-shirt with a blasting rocket ship decal on it. The shirt was too small for him: a slice of his belly stuck out, and the sleeves rode up over the muscles in his arms.

"Would you look at that?" Mr. Cappabianco

said. He took the baseball cap off his head and put it on Valentine's. It was red and had a white patch sewn on it. "I Amaze Myself," it said. Valentine took the hat off and adjusted the plastic strap to fit his head.

"Almost time to go," Carly said. "Are you pumped?"

"I'm ready," said Valentine.

"You look great," I told him, and it was true. I'd never thought of Valentine as handsome before – he was a Dutchman. But he looked so cute standing there, cute and confused and excited. *Wait!* I wanted to say. *Don't go! Stay here in New Wilmington with me. We'll both be Amish. I'll join your church, and we'll get married so you can keep your pay. Your mother can teach me to make quilts and I'll be the daughter she never had.* I didn't say any of this, of course. Valentine was saying, "Let's go."

"We are out of here," Carly said. When I didn't follow them out the door, she added, "Aren't you coming, Sookey?"

"I don't think I will," I told her. "I think I'll just stick around here until you get back."

"Suit yourself," she said. "An hour to Pittsburgh, another hour until his bus comes, then an hour back home."

"I'll be here when you get back," I said. "Maybe I'll clean up while you're gone."

Carly said, "I'll tell you all about it." She said, "Daddy's going to let me drive!"

So it was five o'clock. I rinsed out Mr.

Cappabianco's beer cans so they wouldn't stink up the garbage. I emptied ashtrays and washed them. I swept up Valentine's hair with a broom and a dust pan, and flushed it down the toilet, then I ran the vacuum cleaner. I even washed Valentine's Dutchman clothes before putting them into a plastic trash bag. Then I knotted the bag and threw it in the garbage. Soon, it was six fifty-eight. I was dusting. Lemon-scented furniture polish. I doubted the place had been dusted since Mrs. Cappabianco left. The phone rang, and I answered it: "Cappabianco residence."

A woman's voice said, "This is Sarah with the F. B. I. Valentine Byler's buggy was found in the woods. Do you know where he is?"

I said yes.

I spilled everything.

I was a traitor.

A Judas.

It wasn't until later, replaying this conversation in my head that I realized people affiliated with the F. B. I. wouldn't refer to themselves as "Sarah with the F. B. I." Nor would they speak so slowly, liltingly, with an unmistakable Amish Dutch accent.

Valentine's mother.

One of the things that people like about New Wilmington is its quaintness. Old ladies from Pittsburgh charter the buses that bring them here to shop at the Christmas Village, browse at Sherwood Florist, eat Chinese food at the Olde Wok Inne, and

Expatriates

aim their cameras at the Amish Dutch. Mostly, they get shots of blue-coated backsides because the Amish consider photographs to be graven images. What the Pittsburgh ladies want, however, are pictures of posed and smiling Amish faces, pictures of themselves sitting next to a Dutchman in his buggy.

Not long ago, one Pittsburgh lady got lucky: she snapped a picture of Valentine's father, Andy R. Byler, standing in the doorway of Frank Whiting's diner, sucking on a Swisher Sweet. That picture got made into a postcard, a best-selling postcard that you can buy at Geraldine Miller's Five and Dime.

A good way to torment Andy R. is to send him a bunch of those postcards. Everyone thought Chick Cappabianco was behind this: a postcard a day, every day, for months and months. Some with Andy R.'s face scribbled out. Some with a moustache added to his upper lip. Some with glasses drawn around his eyes. Some with a big heart circling his face.

I knew it was Carly. Getting even. She was so good at revenge.

After Valentine jumped the fence, every single one of Mr. Cappabianco's Amish employees up and quit. None of the Dutchmen wanted to work for him. Not even regular people would. Mr. Cappabianco was as shady and sinister as they'd always expected. A dago. A pervert who lured innocent Amish boys away from their families. He was left filling all his pallet orders by himself. Carly helped him. They worked late into the night: you could hear the air compressor running and the guns stamping nails into the boards. You could hear country music playing on their radio. You could hear them laughing or cussing at each other. I could hear everything from my bedroom, where I sat alone.

Banished.

In exile.

I wasn't there helping the Cappabiancos nail pallets because I wasn't allowed to go over there anymore.

At eleven o'clock, Ascension Day night, my father, with his goatee and his navy blue Dockers, and his white turtle neck, looked down on me and said, "Sookey, what the hell were you thinking?"

My mother said, "His poor mother. What she must be going through."

"But it's what he wanted," I told them. "He said so. Doesn't that count?"

"He wouldn't have wanted it," my father said, "had he not been exposed to those people. He's Amish, for Christ's sake. He doesn't have any job skills."

"He knows how to nail pallets," I said.

"Sheriff Chamberlain is coming over here," my father said. "In half an hour. You'd better sit down and think about this. You'd better get your story straight because you're going to tell him everything."

"Everything?"

"That's right. Everything Carly and her father did."

"But what about what I did?"

My mother said, "You didn't do that much, Sookey. What you did, your confession will cancel out. But for now, you'd better not go over there. We don't want you to be any more implicated, do we?"

"It might be a little late for that," I said. "I'm pretty implicated."

My father said, "You'd better rethink your choice of friends."

So I told. Everything. Same as I'm telling you. My heart was pounding, my palms were sweating. This was the worst thing I'd ever done in my life, and my parents were disappointed in me, and the sheriff was on his way over here in the middle of the night, and when he got here, a confession would be forcibly extracted out of me. I was making decisions! I was making sacrifices! I was forsaking the Cappabiancos in favor of the truth! I was cleansing my conscience. I thought I could go to jail. And for one brief and glowing moment, all attention focused on me. I knew all the answers to all the questions. I thought that confessing would feel like love.

Sheriff Chamberlain showed up around midnight, sleepy and stretching. He scribbled down some of the details. "Greyhound in Pittsburgh" was one of them; "Colorado" was another. "The kid is seventeen years old," he said. "Eighteen in August. This happens every so often, a Dutch kid jumping the fence. He'll be back." Tucking his note pad in his coat pocket, he added, "The big problem here is that this usually sets off a chain reaction. One Dutch kid leaves, and this gives another the idea to leave. It's known as the Domino Effect."

"So what are you going to do?" I asked.

"Chick Cappabianco and his girl deny everything," he said. "It's your word against theirs. What can I do?" He shrugged. "Really I don't have to do anything at all. This town will take care of that."

Three weeks later, I was in summer school – Daddy thought I had too much idle time on my hands – and I was sitting in Frank Whiting's diner, reading *Hamlet*. Act IV, Scene 3. The King keeps asking Hamlet what he's done with Polonius's body, and Hamlet's being real evasive about it. Finally, Hamlet says to go look for Polonius in heaven, and if he's not there, in a month or so, you "shall nose him as you go up the stairs into the lobby." Meaning the rank and foul stench of his decaying body will lead you to where he is. I was marking this line with a yellow highlighter pen when Carly Cappabianco slid into the booth across from me. She pushed a postcard across the table without saying a word. It had a picture of some filthy-looking bearded old hippie man squinting into the sun and holding a bulging marijuana cigarette. "A Rocky Mountain Hi," it said.

"That looks exactly like Andy R.," I said. It

was the first thing that popped into my head. "Except for the tie dye."

"Doesn't it, though?" agreed Carly. "It really is an uncanny resemblance."

We both got quiet just then. I was waiting for Carly to tell me off: whatever I had coming, I deserved. Only she just leaned back and smiled at me a little, like she knew I was nervous and she thought it was cute. She wasn't going to tell me off. She'd made the first move by coming here, and she was leaving the rest up to me.

"So Valentine made it," I said. I longed to flip the card over and see what he'd written to her. But I didn't. It wasn't any of my business anymore.

"He made it," Carly said. "He's working at a sawmill somewhere outside Denver."

"As long as he's happy," I said. "I guess that's what's important."

"I guess," said Carly.

There were so many things I could've said just then. *Have you heard from your mother, Carly? Do you miss R.T.? Are those calluses on your hands from building pallets?* All I had to do was ask, and I know she would've answered me. I know she would've started to talk. I could've said, *About Valentine*, and she would've said, *Forget about it.* It's just that when you've done something that you know is bad and wrong, the last thing you want is the party you've hurt to be so easily forgiving. You want to be punished; you want to do penance. You don't want to hear Carly Cappabianco say, "Susan, I forgive you."

The Fifth Mrs. Hughes

My mother had a stack of clippings she cut out of women's magazines – *Family Circle, Good Housekeeping, Redbook.* She brought them home from the Lawrence County Center for Behavioral Health where she's a receptionist. She's been reprimanded – "Spoken to," she says – twice for interfering with the patients. She calls it "giving advice."

She fanned the clippings out on the table in front of me. "Hair do's," she explained. She heard that my father and his fourth wife had separated. She was vague about her sources. "You haven't done a thing with your hair since that baby was born," my mother said. "Now, I found some styles that would look very nice on you, Lillian, and I also found some that would not become you at all. Let's see if you can tell which are which."

She'd trimmed closely around the models' heads. No necks. No bodies. Just hair, piled high. The clippings reminded me of how I used to cut outfits out of the Sears' catalogue, entire wardrobes for my paper dolls, how furious I became when I couldn't get a purple gown to fit exactly over the yellow-haired doll. It was a problem my father solved by chopping off her arms.

My hair is all one length, long and straight, and parted down the middle. With the exception of a home perm that gave it the texture of cotton candy, I've worn it this way since I was six years old. The coffee was still dripping, I hadn't showered yet, the baby would be up any minute, and my mother, dressed right down to her shoes, was smiling at me from across the table.

"Well?" she said. "Which are which?"

I told her I had no idea.

"The third Mrs. Hughes has bangs," she said. My mother had been the first, the *original* Mrs. Hughes. "But she's still in her thirties. Do you think menopausal women can get away with bangs?"

"You look fine, Mom, the way you are."

"You could highlight your hair," she said. "It can look very natural. It's something to keep in mind. You can do it yourself. Lemon juice."

"Red light," I warned.

"The early bird may get the worm, Lillian," my mother said, "but it's the second mouse who gets the cheese. When I get home from work tonight, let's give each other bangs."

Thirteen is a lucky number for a fetus: too late for a fickle girl to still consider that other option. Living in a college dorm full of menstruating women, three months went by, and I ignored what I had missed. When I lived at home, my period came on the same day as my mother's. It was as if I needed her body to know my own.

"What are you going to do about this?" my mother said when I called her. I was in Philadelphia; my mother was in New Castle, on the other side of the state, close to the Ohio line. I wasn't in love, so I came home. The boy was a blur, a body in a bed in a fraternity house. I left without telling him.

I named my daughter Justine, but my mother doesn't call her that. My mother calls the baby Bill. She says she doesn't remember her own baby costing so much, but then she never used disposable diapers with stick 'em tabs. No, she diapered me in the thick padded cloth that later made excellent dust rags, and she nursed me, too. She told me that all it took to let down her milk was hearing a baby cry – and not just her own baby, either. This happened for any baby, anywhere. At the market. In church. On television.

"Really?" I teased. "On television?"

Her hand fluttered over her chest. "Maybe not on television," she said. "That might be a bit of an exaggeration. How often do you hear babies crying on television?"

"Still," she continued. "I couldn't stop it from happening. Not even when I tried. I was forever walking around with wet spots on my shirt."

The Fifth Mrs. Hughes

Into the eighth month of my pregnancy, my milk came in, and I had to layer cotton pads in my bras. My mother told me that her milk came in during her seventh month when she was carrying me, and that my father thought she was really something. She said there was this time when Daddy reached for her in the middle of the night, and her milk squirted across the room, and he laughed. He said, "You should enter a contest."

"Like you were a cow," I told her. I was feeling that way myself. Slow-moving. Unblinking. My jaw constantly grinding. I couldn't imagine the sex that had gotten me in this situation; I couldn't picture myself ever having sex again. "One of those blue-ribbon heifers he'd seen at the county fair."

Wrong conclusion.

My mother still thinks of this as some great compliment, proof of her womanliness.

But Justine is a bottle baby – I'd been too impatient, too squeamish – to breast feed, and though my mother harps that formula isn't cheap, and the cost is coming out of her purse, I don't think she really minds. We're both light sleepers, and for those middle-of-the-night feedings, I find myself waking before the baby, but not always before my mother.

The baby sleeps in my bedroom, in this beautiful oak crib we picked up at a garage sale – as soon as we stripped off the tacky yellow paint and stained the wood a deep cherry, it was like brand new – and about two weeks after she was born, I opened my eyes, and there was my mother standing over her, warm bottle ready, before she even had a chance to cry.

I closed my eyes and made my breathing slow and heavy. My mother was humming – softly; she didn't want to wake me – as she tiptoed out of my bedroom and across the hall to hers, baby in her arms.

I watched the numbers on my clock change. Eleven minutes went by before I got up and stood in her doorway. My mother had the baby nestled in bed with her, the empty bottle on the nightstand, and the baby's lips pursed around her pinky finger. She said, "I didn't think you were awake."

My mother is a small, thin woman, and her walk is stiff, as if someone duct-taped a curtain rod to her back, but there in her bed, her body – arms, legs, spine – curved gently around the baby. "I can take her, Mom," I said. I meant to sound willing and accountable. I'm nineteen years old. It still came out more like an apology.

"No need for that," she said. "We're fine. She'll be sleeping again in no time. You go on back to bed."

"You sure?"

"Absolutely," she said. But as I was turning away, she added, "Unless you'd like to come get in with us."

So I did. And this has been our routine for the past five months: we all go to our own beds at different times, and we all end up in my mother's bed around three o'clock. I think my mother likes having a full bed again.

The Fifth Mrs. Hughes

You can know too much about the lives your parents led, about your father's character and your mother's desires. "Things between Daddy and me were fine," my mother whispered in bed late one night, still puzzled. She was stroking Justine's cheek. "We were happy. Then you were born and everything changed."

I was six years old when my father moved out, and there are certain things I remember about living with him. He liked to cook, but he had to muscle his way into my mother's kitchen because his meals were so bad and his messes so big. He added ketchup to spaghetti, sour cream to meatloaf, pineapple chunks to mashed potatoes, and when in doubt, he doused everything with Italian salad dressing. "This tastes disgusting," he'd say, and then we'd go to Friendly's for banana splits.

My father is a tall man with a thick stomach and skinny legs. He prefers calling information to looking up numbers in the phone book, listening to Ella Fitzgerald to watching the news. Balancing the checkbook was my mother's job. He didn't believe that children should be hit, not even a smack on the hand, nor should they be made to tie their shoes. He believed that children would eventually potty train themselves; they would go to bed when they were tired enough.

He was thirty-six years old when I was born, and he thought we were both terribly oppressed.

Parenthood was a window painted shut, he said, and childhood was a door that locked from the outside. I didn't quite understand him, and neither did my mother. She wanted another baby. She divorced my father when he finally admitted that a few months after my birth, instead of going on that fishing trip to Florida, he'd had a vasectomy.

My mother didn't need me to give her bangs; a few days later, she came home from work with them. "One of Dr. Young's is a stylist," she said, "in addition to being an obsessive-compulsive sex addict. What do you think?" She was fluffing them with her fingers.

Her bangs were too short, puffy and high on her forehead. They made her look fierce. "Very nice," I said. "Only it'll take forever to grow them out. The question is, do you like them?"

Justine was in her highchair, and I was feeding her applesauce. Every time the baby opened her mouth, my mother's mouth opened, too. "Bill likes pears," she said. "There's a jar in the cupboard."

"Next time," I said.

"Whatever," said my mother, but she got out the pears anyway and another spoon and pulled up a chair beside the baby. "I understand the separation between your father and the fourth Mrs. Hughes is a legal one," she said, "not the kind where he moves in with Aunt Patty for a few weeks."

The Fifth Mrs. Hughes

"How do you know these things?"

Justine turned her head, rejecting the applesauce, but accepting the pears. My mother was cooing at her. "Mommy's going to do Grandma a favor, Bill."

"What's that?"

"She's going to call Grandpa and invite him over for dinner."

"No, I'm not," I said. "I'm not getting myself involved with anything of the sort."

My mother winked at the baby. "She'll change her mind." Her tone was confidential. "Every child of divorce longs for the day when her parents get back together."

When I finally gave in and accepted that I was pregnant, my mother was not the first person I called. My father was. I thought he'd be easier to tell, easier to deal with. He wasn't paying my tuition; his house wasn't where I'd go. The fourth Mrs. Hughes answered the telephone.

After his divorce from my mother, my father took up with, and occasionally married, a series of women who had problems. Alcoholic ex-husbands. Crazy ex-boyfriends. Bankruptcies and bad credit, minimum wage jobs and custody battles. Violent teenage sons and dyslexic sons and daughters with eating disorders. The only kind of woman he seemed to attract were the ones who knew how to file restraining orders and how to apply for food stamps and how to file a claim and collect a settlement for slipping on an icy sidewalk in front of a supermarket.

"Don't you know any nice women?" I asked him once. "Normal women?"

"Like who?" he wanted to know.

"Elementary school teachers or nurses or somebody's sister."

"A woman like your mother," he mused. "Do you know any?"

I had to admit I didn't.

"Well, then," he said. "I guess it's settled. I'm disappointed in you, Lily. These women are human beings. They have hard luck just like the rest of us. It's not your place to judge them."

Linda, the fourth Mrs. Hughes, insisted that the nasty fall she took in front of Giant Eagle was the reason for her back trouble. A settlement was pending. She was a chunky woman with arms as thick as a man's and hair the color of a doorknob. She was also the friendliest woman my father ever married. "Oh, Lily," she said. "I'll put him on right away, sweetheart. He's been acting depressed lately, and he'll be so thrilled you called."

My father's voice over the telephone is much deeper than it is in person. "What about a clinic?" he was asking. "What kind of services are available to you? I can drive out there, you know. Leave New Castle now and be there in about six hours and get you through this."

"Too late for that, Dad."

The Fifth Mrs. Hughes

"Okay, that's all right," he said. "Let me ask you this: do you love him? Your boyfriend? That's assuming you know who he is, and you know I don't mean that in a judgmental way, Lily."

"The boy was a body in a bed in a frat house, Dad," I said.

"Does he know? Have you told him?"

I said I hadn't.

"Good. Don't," my father said. "Because that's a mess you don't want to get mixed up in, what with custody and paternity tests and fathers' rights. It can be hellish. Especially if you don't care for the guy. Reet?"

"Right." When I was little, he and my mother had joint custody of me. She'd never given him any trouble – not even during the stretch when he didn't pay child support – so I wasn't sure what or whose hell he was referring to. Maybe that of the second Mrs. Hughes. Her name was Carol Anne and they were married for less than a year. What little I remember about her was the way she hid the Fig Newtons when I came to visit, saying she'd bought them with her own money, and they were meant for her kids' lunches. It was a logic that made sense to me; I didn't take it personally, but my father did.

"Then I'm going to be a grandfather," he was saying. "That's great. That's fine. I have some news for you, too, baby doll." He cleared his throat and lowered his voice. "I've proposed to a wonderful woman and she said yes. I'm engaged."

"You're already married, Dad," I said.

"There's no need to point out the obvious, is there?"

I said I guessed not.

"It's just going to take some time. A year, maybe more. She also has a prior commitment. You'll be so pleased for me, I know. Just don't tell your mother, whatever you do. She already thinks I'm a fool. A reasonable request, agreed?"

"Agreed," I said.

"It's too bad about the guy, Lily," my father said. "I'd be happier for you had loved him. Even if he didn't love you and you just loved him, I'd feel better. Are you seeing anyone now?"

"I'm pregnant, Dad."

"And? So? Look, just keep in touch. Call me when you get home," he said. "Call me when the baby's born."

The third Mrs. Hughes was twenty-four years old when she met my father. Her name was Melissa. She was a birdy little woman, with fly-away blond hair and bangs. She was the mother of five scrawny children. She'd lived in the same duplex as my father.

One night, her boyfriend beat her up and left her propped up against the washing machine on the front porch. My father called the police, and when they showed up, one cop used his flashlight to lift the hair off her face so the other cop could take her picture. It made my father furious. "Don't treat her like she's a couch or a mud flap or a spider web," he shouted. "She's a human being, goddamn it!"

They were married three weeks later, and they stayed married for ten years. Her oldest son is about to graduate from high school, and he still calls my father Dad.

My mother was running water to give Justine a bath. "I don't understand you, Lillian," she said. "One simple request. All I'm asking is that you give him a call and invite him over. Tell him I'm making Salisbury steak and mashed potatoes, he'll love that. I'd just like to spend some time with him before he gets married again. Is that asking too much?"

She'd caught me off guard. "Where did you hear that?" I said. Not once over the past year did my father mention his engagement to me again. At least, not explicitly. When I helped him move out of Linda's house and into an apartment, he'd smiled at me like we were conspirators, and he'd mentioned that early October is the prettiest time of year in western Pennsylvania, and wouldn't it be wonderful to celebrate joy and love in early October, what with the golden sunshine and the red and yellow and orange leaves. "Is that something you've heard, Mom, that he's getting married?"

She sighed and plunked the baby in the tub. "It's just his usual pattern. Your father is fifty-six years old, Lillian, and he's not used to living on his own. He needs love and companionship, same as any one else. Hand me a washcloth," she said.

"The one with the lambs. Bill likes that one."

In the thirteen years that my parents have been divorced, my mother never got serious with another man. She rarely even went out on a date. When she did, I waited up for her. She always came home in time to catch the eleven o'clock news, and we'd sit on the couch, and she'd tell me about the man's bad breath or his filthy car or the stingy tip he left the waitress. She'd sit cross-legged, eating nectarines as if they were a cure.

"I don't know why this is so important to you, Mom," I said. "Do you think you and Dad have a chance, really? Why would you even want him? He lies, he cheats. He's a mess. He's a terrible husband. There are three other woman who'd agree with that."

My mother handed me a towel. "Your baby has a wet head," she told me. "You'd better dry off her hair."

She told me about when she met my father, how they'd left a party, both of them a bit drunk, and he took her for a ride on his ten-speed. He was twenty-five years old; she was nineteen. They were at the top of the Jefferson Street Hill, the steepest, longest hill in town, and she sat on the handlebars with her eyes closed and she didn't open them until they were at the bottom.

I thought about Bill's father, the clean break from him, my detachment, how easy it was to reduce him to a body in a bed. I wish I could say there was a happy ending to this. I did call for my mother, but my father wasn't home. He was out getting Chinese food. Melissa, the third Mrs. Hughes, picked up the phone. "Lily," she said, "it's so great to hear your voice. Peter says he told you. About us, I mean. We never should have gotten divorced in the first place. It was my fault, really. I'm lucky he still wants me. But I'm babbling. You have a baby! We both do! I have a little boy who's about six months old. We have to get the kids together soon. Do you want Peter to call you when he gets in?"

"Red light," I told my mother, and she nodded, like it was what she expected. "It's late," she said. "Going on nine o'clock. Let's put Bill to bed."

I said, "Let's all go to bed."

I drifted in and out of sleep to look at my mother and my daughter as they slept. I touched their cheeks and smoothed their eyebrows and petted their hair. My mother's bangs feathered across her forehead; Justine's head was sweaty along her hairline. We were huddled so close together that I thought I was running my fingers through my mother's hair until I pushed through a tangle and realized it was my own hair I'd been touching. I was thinking about when I was little, climbing into bed with my mother and father. It's safe and it's warm and it's nothing like love, nothing as unreliable as that.

Schandorsky's Mother

Schandorsky didn't see his mother jump into Elder's Pond, but he heard the splash. "Yo, Schandorsky," somebody said. "Your mother's in the water." He watched his mother paddle to the bank, her clothes clinging to her shape; she slicked back her hair like a woman in a perfume commercial. "Hey, Schandorsky," somebody said. "You think your mother would want to go out sometime?"

"You could ask," he said.

Schandorsky lives with his mother. There is no father. There is a family album, though, of photos of his infant self held by various people. To those who don't know differently, it might appear that these people are relatives, but they are not. An overwhelming need to provide some semblance of security overtook Schandorsky's mother shortly after his birth. The last bit of her college savings bought the camera as well as the album. For several years, in grocery stores, in the park and at the circus – wherever a kind-hearted stranger tickled

Schandorsky's chin and told his mother he was cute – they were offered the opportunity to hold him if they agreed to pose for a picture. The smiles of these people are puzzled, but accommodating.

"This is your family," Schandorsky's mother told him. "See this old guy? Your Grandpa Lyle. A doctor. The old lady beside him who's holding you, that's your Grandma Dot. This boy is your uncle. His name is Will and he goes to college somewhere."

Flipping through the album, Schandorsky's mother pointed to the places on other people's faces where he could find parts of his own: the small lobes of his ears, a high forehead, dimples, brown eyes like his. His mother's illusions might have worked had they lived in a big city, but as Schandorsky got older, he remembered the things she told him. He thought he recognized his family in stores and parking lots and on the street. He was hurt when they didn't recognize him in return.

"We're black sheep," his mother explained. "Our family doesn't like something I did." She thought it would be best to move out of their little hometown and into another one, and she stopped taking pictures.

Schandorsky's mother has many male admirers. They are interested in Schandorsky in so far as it seems to please his mother. His favorite is a logger named Charlie who has a Harley Davidson tattoo on his upper arm. "A damn bike I used to have," says Charlie. He has a tattoo on his wrist with the word *Mary* in the middle. "That's for me," says Schandorsky's mother, whose name is Nancy. "He wants me to marry him."

"Will you?" says Schandorsky.

"I doubt it."

Schandorsky is disappointed. He likes when Harley Charlie pulls into their driveway in his pick-up. His clothes are covered with sawdust; he takes off his boots on the porch, dumping sawdust on the flowerbed. His hair is curly and wild and leaves and twigs are caught in it like a bird's nest. Sometimes, after school, Harley Charlie will give him a ride to the diner in his pick-up and Tony DePaulo from the seventh grade can't mess with him then. "Why won't you marry him?"

"I think he's already married," his mother says.

"Too bad," says Schandorsky. Harley Charlie divides the world into tree huggers and tree killers. Schandorsky would have enjoyed telling people that his dad is a tree killer with a chain saw. "Too bad."

"Not really," his mother says. "He says 'damn' too much. Plus, he's very messy."

Schandorsky's mother waitresses at the town diner. She has to wear her hair pulled back into a pony tail; this style makes her look rather young. When tourists see Schandorsky sitting at the counter doing his homework, they think he is their waitress's little brother. For those who mention this thought, Schandorsky's mother is efficient: she gives them a napkin and an extra slice of bread. In between orders, Schandorsky's mother sits beside

Schandorsky's Mother

him, smoking cigarettes, sipping coffee, and turning pages. She likes to read poetry; so much, in fact, that all her reading has prompted her to begin a poem of her own – one that chronicles her courtship with Schandorsky's father. "So someday you'll understand," she tells him. She lets him read what she's done so far:

Part One

> Your denim black with grease and dirt under
> > your nails
> Your skin sweats stale beer and stale smoke
>
> Leaning against the white walls of my bed
> > room
> You might be a bruise
>
> You might be a blemish
> You might be a stain on my virgin sheets

"Did he work at a gas station?" Schandorsky asks. He might like to work in a gas station some day. He likes the smell. He likes cars and trucks. He can imagine his father pulling up to the pumps in a pick-up like Harley Charlie's. "Fill'er up," his father would say, and Schandorsky would nod, tapping his toe as he squeezes the pump, squinting into the sun.

"No," his mother says. "He didn't work at a gas station. But he sure did look as though he might have."

> You clog up my mother's toilet
> Leave scum on the sides of her tub
>
> Make me cry tears of acid rain
> You want me to go with you
>
> My dress is white and unsuitable for travel
> If I go, I will shower, change into something
>   else
> Pack my curling iron and my S.A.T. study
>   guide
> Make arrangements for the children I babysit
>
> Bring Bactine to squirt on our cuts
> Come get me

Acid rain, as Schandorsky is learning in Mrs. Ferguson's third grade science class, is not a good thing. But the rest of the poem does not surprise him: his mother is very touchy about the bathroom. Plugging up the pot with toilet paper and candy bar wrappers had her very upset. He's about to ask her about those kids she used to know, but Ray, the cook, is dinging the bell and hollering, "Order up!"

It's Friday night, and Harley Charlie is taking them to an auction in Butler, a town about two hours away. "There'll be farm equipment," he promises. "And animals. And household goods."

Schandorsky's Mother

Schandorsky is sitting in between his mother and Harley Charlie. His mother teases the tree killer, calling him "Chuckie" and "Charles" and "Chaz."

"Damn woman," says Harley Charlie, smiling. "Don't call me those butt-buddy names."

"Harley Charlie," she says.

"My wild youth. Those crazy days," he says. "But not anymore. You would know what I mean."

"Not me," says Schandorsky's mother.

Harley Charlie shows Schandorsky how to drive a stick shift. "This is first," he says. "This is second." His hand is over Schandorsky's as they guide the stick. "That's it," he says. "Get a feel for it." The motor revs and the truck slows down. "No, son, you got'er in neutral."

"Neutral," says Schandorsky's mother.

"Neutral," says Harley Charlie. "Like you. Damn Neutral Nancy's what I'm going to call you." He laughs and reaches behind Schandorsky to squeeze his mother's shoulder.

"That's me," she says.

"I like it," Harley Charlie says. "Nancy'd be a nice middle name, I think."

"Charlene Nancy?" she asks.

"What are you talking about?" Schandorsky says. He leans his head back against Harley Charlie's arm, making the tree killer have to move it.

"Names," his mother says. "What girl names do you like?"

"None," says Schandorsky. "I don't like girls."

Harley Charlie says, "You will one of these days."

"Never," says Schandorsky.

His mother says, "You might have to sooner than you think."

The auction is crowded and dusty. They eat hot sausage sandwiches and cherry pie. Although the service is slow and insolent, Schandorsky's mother insists on leaving a sizable tip. "I can relate," she tells them.

Before the bidding starts, they walk around looking at tractors and manure spreaders, pigs and cows, old dining room suites. Harley Charlie wants to buy Schandorsky's mother a new bed.

"What's wrong with the one she's got?" Schandorsky wants to know.

"She needs a bigger one," Harley Charlie says. "She's still growing, you know."

Schandorsky's mother says, "Who, me?"

They look at old books and magazines, colored glass bottles and tarnished silverware. "Look," cries Schandorsky's mother. "My parents had china in this same pattern." The set of plates and teacups has blue flowers and is trimmed in gold.

"It's pretty," says Harley Charlie. "Is it worth much?"

"Probably," says Schandorsky's mother. "But it's worth more to me and you don't have to pay for it." She locates the owner and buys the china as well as a champagne glass, paying him with her tip money.

Harley Charlie doesn't find a bed he likes,

Schandorsky's Mother

but he does buy a load of hay for his horses. As he loads it on his truck, Schandorsky's mother runs her finger around the gold trim on a plate. Then, she throws it like a frisbee, and it breaks against the brick of the auction office building. This strikes her as funny, so she does it again, this time sending a saucer into orbit. "You try," she suggests, so Schandorsky throws a teacup, and his mother giggles, apparently delighted.

Harley Charlie finishes loading just as they're down to the last dinner plate. "Would you care to do the honors?" says Schandorsky's mother. Her cheeks are pink; her eyes, bright.

"It's fun," Schandorsky says.

"What's the matter with you?" says Harley Charlie, sticking his hands in his pockets. "Why would you break up that damn china that you had to have so bad and that you spent so much money on?"

"I bought it," Schandorsky's mother said. She juts out her chin and says, "It was mine to do with as I pleased." Pulling the champagne glass out of a plastic bag, she says, "I bought a little something for you, too. You can do with it as you please." She holds up the glass, and Schandorsky can see it says, HAPPY 10th ANNIVERSARY! "I know someone you can take this home to," says Schandorsky's mother. She hands Harley Charlie the glass and climbs in the truck.

"You think you're pretty damn cute," he mutters. "Want to break one more glass, boy?" he asks Schandorsky.

Schandorsky nods. "I guess." But somehow, it's not as satisfying. The ride home is quiet, and when Schandorsky's sleeping head lands on his mother's shoulder, she shrugs him off.

After school, Schandorsky goes to the diner and his mother slides a bowl of beef barley soup in front of him. She's in a bad mood, she tells him – but not because of anything he did. She says she's mad at Harley Charlie. "How come?" Schandorsky wants to know.

"Because when he makes a mess, he doesn't help clean it up," she says. "At least, not the way you're supposed to. What'd you do in school?"

"What mess?" He doesn't like this soup; the barley reminds him of the maggots he saw when Tony DePaulo held him upside down in a garbage can. He pushes the bowl away, and his mother pushes it back. "Was it a big mess?"

"Never mind," his mother tells him. "I worked some on my poem today. You can read it while I fill the salt and pepper shakers."

Part Two

Your motorcycle buzzes like an angry bee
As we fly down highways searching for
    flowers

Schandorsky's Mother

Instead, we find broken whiskey bottles
       and used condoms
Still damp with spirit and seed

"Don't hold me so tight," you say
But I'm afraid I might fall off

"Lean the way I lean," you say
So I close my eyes and I obey

Lightning flashes, brief and sudden
Followed by the applause of thunder and the
       encore of rain

It may be dangerous to ride during a storm
But I haven't bathed in three or four or five
       days

"You didn't take a bath in how many days?" says Schandorsky. He can't believe it. She makes him take a bath every night whether he needs one or not. He tells her, "You make me take a bath every damn night, and you didn't take one in how many days?"

"Shut up!" his mother says. She'd been filling the shakers in the booth where Ruth Becktal, the town busybody, is sitting. "Watch your language, too. You sound like a gutter mouth like someone else I know." She forces a smile at Ruth. "He's got imagination," she says. "I don't know where he gets it."

My pink coat smells like stale beer
It smells like stale smoke

We eat supper at a convenience store
A pack of Starburst for you and a Milky
    Way for me

We drink beer and play darts in a dive on a
    Sunday
Tattooed people know us by our Christian
    names

I lost my curling iron, my study guide, my
    right to white
I don't know where I'm going

Schandorsky glares at his mother. She's sneezing over salt and pepper shakers. He knows where he's going. He's going to the candy counter to help himself to a pack of Starburst and a Milky Way bar. "No more damn maggot soup for me," he says.

Schandorsky's mother isn't feeling well. She's tired all the time. When Harley Charlie comes over, she says, "Not tonight, Chuckie." When Schandorsky tells her he's not taking any damn bath, she just sighs and tells him to wash his hands and his face, his neck and his arms. "Give me a kiss, Albert," she says, holding out her arms. Schandorsky hasn't kissed his mother since the argument they had about eating a popsicle while sitting on the toilet. His mother told him it was a yucky, germy thing to do, and Schandorsky told her so was kissing.

"Yuck," he says now. "There's no way I'm kissing you."

After school, Schandorsky sees Harley Charlie's pick-up pulled up along side the curb. He runs toward the truck, but stops when he sees Georgie Wayne from the second grade throwing his backpack in it. He watches Harley Charlie do a U-turn, then drive down the street. Georgie Wayne is bouncing up and down in the passenger seat.

When Schandorsky gets to the diner, he sees a banner: HAPPY B-DAY, NANCY. It is his mother's birthday. Her co-workers present her with a cake illuminated by twenty-six candles. All day long, regulars and customers alike have wished Schandorsky's mother a happy birthday and tipped her extra. Not that she deserved it. She's been moody and clumsy and forgetful. When a tourist asks for a B. L. T, Schandorsky's mother says, "Would you like mayo on that?"

"No," says the tourist. "I would like bacon, lettuce, and tomato."

"No shit," says Schandorsky's mother. She drops her order pad and sits down at the counter, beside Schandorsky. "I'm wiped out," she says, explaining her treatment of the tourist. "Just exhausted. Plus, I have a crampy belly. Hurts."

Instead of her usual black coffee, she is sipping orange juice through a straw. J. R. Green is sitting next to her, puffing on a cigar, and she waves away the smoke. "What did you do today?" she asks Schandorsky.

He says, "Gave Tony DePaulo two dollars so he wouldn't put me in a garbage can."

His mother puts her hands over her eyes. "Did you have a good day at school?"

He says, "No. I hate that damn school." He thinks of Georgie Wayne bouncing up and down in Harley Charlie's truck.

His mother only sighs. "I finished my poem during my break," she says. "You want to see it?"

Schandorsky waivers between the desire to hurt his mother's feelings and the desire not to hurt her feelings. He's angry with her, but he doesn't know exactly why. She doesn't look like she feels so good. She rocks back and forth, clutching her stomach. "Let's see the damn poem," he says.

Part Three

I hear singing

> Early in the morning I wake to find you
> cross-legged in front of the television
> hypnotized by cartoons
> A cigarette balances on the line between
>   your lips
> and you croon Fred Flintstone's song
> "Billy?"

Schandorsky's Mother

"His name is Billy?" says Schandorsky scornfully. He would kick a kid's ass for having a butt-buddy name like Billy.

"He called himself Bill," Schandorsky's mother says. "But to me, he was always Billy."

> Your eyes never leave the screen
> "Yeah?"
> The sheets are stained red
> "Billy?"
> And for a minute I rejoice in relief
> "Waddaya want?"
> Until I remember last night's spilled red
>   wine
> "Nothing," I say
>
> This is life, I suppose
> Baloney in the fridge and cigarettes and beer
> You have a motorcycle, a police record, and
> $56
> I have nothing
> We drive three kids to Florida in a borrowed
>   car
> to make some money
> The girl carries a baby and a Hershey Bar,
>   Pepsi

"You people ate a lot of junk food," Schandorsky mutters. He notices his mother isn't beside him anymore. She's taking an order. "Shit on a shingle, Ray," she hollers to the kitchen.

"Do you love your baby?" I ask her
Shrugging, she says, "Honey, I got to –
it's gonna look like me."
The boys have $2,000
in a sticky dirty white envelope
They give you half of it
Silently I object
They need it more than you do
You have a home to go to

"Order up," Ray hollers. "Order up." But Schandorsky's mother has disappeared. Ray dings the bell. "Order up, Nancy. Nancy, order up!"

This is love, I suppose
Crunched under you on the floor, the couch,
    the ground
You don't brush your teeth enough
But you buy my cigarettes and you want me
    to smile

"Nag, nag, nag," says Schandorsky. "That's why he's not around. She bugged him about brushing his teeth." This is a feeling Schandorsky is acquainted with only too well.

"Where's Nancy?" Ray is asking. "She's got an order up."

"Yo, Schandorsky," somebody says. "Your

Schandorsky's Mother

mother's in the shit house. Been in there a while. Maybe she jumped in."

       "Remember the first night?" you asked
       You wave a crumpled pack of Salem Light
100's   at me
       as proudly as the American flag
       "I kept this," you say, "because it was
yours."
       I step out of the shower and reach for your
         robe
       when you startle me with a single stolen
white   rose
       I cannot accept your flower, though
       anymore than I can accept this life
       I tell you to take me home

       I hear silence

       "What?" Schandorsky says. "What? Because of a stinking damn flower?"

   His mother appears, wiping her mouth across her sleeve. She looks pale. "I got overheated," she says. "Sorry."

   "You got an order up," Ray says. Pointing at the creamed beef on toast, he says, "It's getting cold."

   "Because of a stinking flower?" says Schandorsky. "You didn't like the damn flower?"

   "Not now, Albert," his mother says. She is looking at the order and shivering. One of her hands grips the counter; the other is pressed against her stomach. It looks as though Schandorsky's mother has been sitting in a big splotch of ketchup. "Take this to table five, Albert," she says, "and you can keep the tip."

"Yo, Schandorsky," somebody says. "What's the matter with your mother?"

"Who knows?" says Schandorsky. He is worried, though, because his mother has just fallen to the floor, and she is moaning and crying.

"Your mother's got a lot on her mind," Harley Charlie tells Schandorsky. They're sitting in his pickup, pulled over to the side of the road so Schandorsky's mother could get some fresh air. She's walking along the edge of Elder's Pond. She only spent one night in the hospital where they informed her that she would be fine. Miscarriages will sometimes happen, and there will be other babies.

"She's going crazy," says Schandorsky. "Damn crazy. She hasn't asked me if I did my homework. She doesn't tell me that sitting too close to the T.V. will ruin my eyes and give me cancer. She hasn't looked in my ears for days."

"Sounds a little crazy," Harley Charlie admits. "Just hang with her, boy. Okay?"

"And," Schandorsky adds, "she made me read this dumb poem she wrote about how she nagged my father and dumped him because she didn't like this flower he gave her." He crosses his arms and waits for Harley Charlie to respond.

Schandorsky's Mother

"I read it," he says. "I guess it's good for all I know about poems. She describes things pretty good, I guess." Harley Charlie is chewing on a pen. "I can't figure your mother out. She should go to night school or something." He grabs Schandorsky's arm and pushes up his shirt sleeve. "You want a tattoo?" he says.

"Okay." His mother won't like it; she'll think the ink will seep into his bloodstream and poison him.

Harley Charlie draws a crescent moon and a series of perfect stars. "I think she misses her family," he's saying. "They don't even know where you all are at. She's got a little brother, too. She thinks he's probably in college somewhere."

Schandorsky says, "You still married?"

"Sort of," says Harley Charlie. "I guess it depends on your mother." He rubs his hand of Schandorsky's tattoo, smudging the ink. Then he dabs his finger on his tongue and rubs away the smears. "There," he says. "All done. You like it?"

"Damn, yes," says Schandorsky. The moon has a nose and eyes and a smile; the stars are shooting all around it. "It would be all right with me if you married my mother."

"Yeah," says Harley Charlie. "It'd be fine with me, too, but it's all up to her. And you know how she is."

Schandorsky reaches for the cigarette Harley Charlie left in the ashtray. He puffs on it and says, "I probably wouldn't expect it to happen if I were you." He's surprised when Harley Charlie laughs and tells him he's probably got that damn right. They look at Schandorsky's mother. She has taken off her shoes and socks, and she's dangling her feet in the water. She's sticking weedy flowers in her hair and tossing rocks in the pond. "Yo, Schandorsky," someone says. "Is that really your mother?"

Schandorsky says, "I think so."

Schandorsky's mother has taken a day off from the diner, so she allows him to have a day off from school. For weeks, she barely spoke to him; she hardly noticed when he was in front of her. When she went to work, she was mean to the customers, and the few who gave her a tip left only a penny or two, just to make a point. On the days she called in sick to work, she sat around the house in her robe, sometimes not moving from the couch for days. Occasionally, a current of life would charge through her index finger, and the channel on the television would change. Harley Charlie stopped by, and although Schandorsky's mother had little to say to him, he gave Schandorsky some money, told him that the rent was taken care of, and promised him his mother would get better. Now, for some reason, it would seem that, today, she is herself. It would seem that Schandorsky's mother can't quit touching him. Her fingers wrap around his earlobes and brush against his hair. While he is standing in front of the refrigerator, looking at some strawberry Jell-O, she sneaks up behind him and captures him in a hug.

Schandorsky's Mother

"Please," says Schandorsky. "Refrain yourself." It's a phrase he learned in science class from Mrs. Ferguson: "Children, please refrain yourselves from talking when I'm talking."

"I can't," his mother says. "I find you irresistible." She takes the jello out of the refrigerator and spoons it out in two bowls.

Schandorsky grunts and curls his lip. His mother is still crazy, but now she's crazy in a different way. She put bananas in the jello. She's talking about jogging in the mornings. She wants to quit smoking. She's on his back about the perils of tooth decay and wearing his clothes to bed so he's already dressed in the morning. "What if there was a fire, and firemen came, and there was a crowd?" she says. "And people saw you were in bed in your school clothes? What would they think?"

Schandorsky says, "They'd think you look pretty stupid in your nightgown and slipper socks." He cuts around the bananas with his spoon and flings them in the sink. "Would you like it better if I slept naked?"

"Smarty pants," his mother says. Her head is bent over her bowl, and her hair falls across her face, shielding her from Schandorsky. "I started thinking today," she says, "about when you were a baby. It was just you and me. So then I started thinking about why I haven't been feeling so hot. About how I need to feel better."

"Yeah?" says Schandorsky. He's interested, but he's not sure he trusts her. He knows that something's been going on, and he knows that he doesn't know all of it.

"I have something for you," she says. "I thought about throwing it away, but I think you should have it." She pulls a paper bag out of her robe pocket.

Schandorsky opens the bag and finds a white stick. One end of the stick has a cover over it, and the other end has a little window with a plus sign on it. Schandorsky rolls his eyes. "What's this darn thing?"

"It's the proof," his mother says, "of the possibility."

"What possibility?"

"Your family," his mother tells him. "It's the proof that there was more of your family. Keep it someplace safe."

Schandorsky promises he will. He will fasten a piece of twine around it and wear it like a necklace under his shirt. He will keep it in the drawer his mother always supplies with fresh socks. He will hang it from the rear view mirror when he is able to drive his own car. The plus sign will fade as he gets older, and as he gets older, he will realize that his mother held this stick between her legs and peed on it because he will hold a stick between his wife's legs as she pees on it. They will be hoping for a plus, praying against a minus, because Schandorsky will already be dreaming of family albums and epic poems.

Many Will Enter, Few Will Win

The mother was a hairdresser, and she ran her beauty shop out of the basement. She wore a long necklace with a gold charm shaped like a pair of scissors. The necklace had been a present from her lover; he often gave her small, but thoughtful gifts: a leather checkbook cover, a brass box for her business cards, a gold-plated spoon for her collection. The mother was a beautiful woman. She wasn't exactly thin – she'd been pregnant twice – but she had coppery red hair and brown eyes and full red lips.

"It's that mouth," the father said. "You can't decide whether you want to kiss it or slap it." He was teasing, although it didn't sound much like teasing. Was telling your wife you wanted to slap her as bad as slapping her? Was telling her you'd thought about kissing her as good as kissing her? The father mulled it over, but could never decide. He and the mother had not made love in five years.

The rubber bands were his idea: wear a thick one tight around your wrist, and have a non-smoker you love, and who loves you, snap it hard whenever you feel the urge to smoke. Both parents smoked: the father, unfiltered Camels; the mother, anything menthol.

There was once a time when the father said that if the price of cigarettes ever went higher than fifty cents a pack, he'd quit. He worked the afternoon shift at a factory that manufactured airplane parts. Management was threatening layoffs, and a pack of cigarettes was now almost three dollars. The mother had said the reason she didn't want to kiss him on the mouth was because his moustache stank.

The father threw away glass ashtrays and plastic ashtrays and ashtrays the mother had made in ceramics class. He threw away eighteen Zippo lighters. Some had been birthday presents; some were for Christmas and Father's Day. The children – a boy and a girl – always bickered over who got to give Dad a Zippo, the one gift he'd be sure to appreciate. There were twelve tins of lighter fluid and several boxes of flints and forty-three plastic lighters, all of them blue. There was a drawer in the kitchen that contained nothing but matchbooks, hundreds and hundreds of them – from gas stations and wedding receptions, from restaurants where the parents had smoked over steak dinners, and from bars where they'd smoked over pitchers of beer. But that was before they were parents.

When the mother was pregnant with the daughter, her panties wouldn't stretch over her hips, and rather than buying larger ones, she took to wearing the father's briefs. She was wobbly, awkward, her belly blown big; her belly was a watermelon, velvety like a tulip, and she was nineteen years old. She crocheted a blanket, squares of ivory and pink.

When she was pregnant with the son, she owned the beauty shop, and her belly was flabby and hard at the same time. She said she couldn't reach her legs to shave them. She wanted the father to do it. The hair on her legs was coarse and dark. There was also hair coming in on her upper lip. She'd been sitting on the toilet seat, wearing the father's briefs, and between her legs, tufts of hair poked out. *What are you staring at?* she'd asked the father.

Some of the matchbooks were from the motel where the mother would go to meet her lover.

The daughter was the non-smoker her father loved. She was a small girl, wiry and quick, and her father called her off the soccer field to snap his rubber band. In the morning, he pounded on the bathroom door while she was in the shower, sweaty and anxious and yelling, "Hurry! Hurry!" He stretched his arm across the supper table when he wanted his rubber band snapped; he held his wrist in front of her face while she was giggling on the telephone. Then there was the day when he pulled her out of the eighth grade while she was taking a geography test. "A family emergency," he told the teacher.

The daughter didn't like snapping her father's rubber band. She liked her father better when he smoked. He channel surfed then, and he drank beer, and he wasn't so restless. He didn't have so much free time. She told him she didn't want to do it anymore, she didn't want to snap his rubber band. "I don't like hurting you," she said.

The father said, "But we only truly learn something when it's painful." He didn't know who the mother's lover was. He'd never seen him. Maybe he was the man who sold her beauty supplies. Maybe she'd met him at the bank or the post office or on the street. Maybe the lover was a non-smoker whose moustache did not stink. The father tried not to think about him.

He told the daughter, "I don't have to take you back to school. We can go out for ice cream. Do you want an ice cream?"

His wrist turned welted and red and bald where there used to be thick blond hair.

The mother's wrist was tiny and pale. She bruised easily so snapping her rubber band would leave a terrible mark. With magic markers borrowed from the son, she colored her rubber band, little squares and triangles of red and orange and yellow. Quitting didn't seem hard for her. She wasn't nervous, like the father. She wasn't gnawing on carrot sticks or chewing gum or biting at her cuticles.

It was because she cheated.

The father knew it, and so did the children,

Many Will Enter, Few Will Win

though through some unspoken agreement, they all acted like they didn't know. They didn't see the lipstick-covered butts floating in the toilet, and they didn't hear the cellophane crackling in the pocket of her bathrobe. They didn't ask why she so often disappeared to the back porch, or why there were butts on the ground next to the rose bushes, or why her breath, when she leaned over to kiss them goodnight, smelled like smoke. When she and the father X-ed off their one hundredth smoke-free day on the calendar, the children applauded and said they were proud.

In the basement beauty shop, the mother stood over the father, shampooing his hair, when he rose, ever-so-slightly, and cupped the gold charm shaped like a pair of scissors in his mouth. He slurped up the long chain to tighten the distance between them. The mother tugged back a bit, a reflex, then waited patiently for him to let go. Her face was close to his – close enough to kiss. She didn't say anything, which made him feel foolish. The scissors clicked against his teeth. The father was a tall and slender man, and his hair was very short and very blond, almost white. The crew cuts the mother gave him made him look sad, like a dandelion with the puff blown off.

When it was time to do the grocery shopping, the mother, once again, said she didn't want to go. She gave the father the checkbook and a list, and she said if he followed the list, he'd do just fine.

She said she had things to take care of at home.

    The last time the father took the children to the grocery store by himself, the son refused to ride in the cart. The father put him in it, and the son climbed out. He insisted on pushing the cart himself, and he made loud motor noises as he took off down the vegetable aisle and around the bend, toward the bakery, while the father was still trying to make sense of the list. Did *bread* mean whole wheat or white? Did *eggs* mean extra-large or jumbo? Milk came in skim, one percent, two percent, and whole: which was right? These seemed like important questions. It seemed important to get them right.

    He had to tell the daughter that the giant claw machine would not work without putting money in it, and no, he wouldn't give her fifty cents because he'd never seen the giant claw pull a stuffed animal out of the pile. "That thing's a rip-off," he said. "It won't work."

    "That's why I need fifty cents," the daughter said. "I want to win a prize."

    He tried to explain that it wasn't so easy. Fifty cents didn't guarantee a stuffed pink pig. Very few people get one, though lots of people try. Many will enter, few will win. That was the point of the giant claw machine.

    The daughter glared at him. "You don't know," she said. She was wearing lipstick and tight denim shorts and the mother's high-heeled clogs. She had on one of the father's shirts, the white one with blue pinstripes; she'd knotted the ends of it

Many Will Enter, Few Will Win

snugly around her waist. She'd cut her bangs herself, using pinking shears, and they lay flat and high on her head. Her bangs were pointy. She looked weird, but also sexy. The father tried a different approach. "I don't have fifty cents," he said.

"That's a lie," she said. "I saw Mom give you money."

"She gave me the checkbook. It's not the same thing."

The son had parked the cart in front of the bakery. There were several old ladies gathered around him, watching him eat a cookie. He grunted like a monkey and scratched his belly, then his head. In the place between where his shorts ended and his cowboy boots began were the hard knobs of his knees. "Let's give him a nickel," the old lady in the lavender pantsuit said.

"Sure," said the son.

"It's not fair," the daughter said.

The one wearing a peach pantsuit smiled and said, "How about another cookie?"

"Yeah," said the son.

"If he gets a cookie, then I should get fifty cents," said the daughter.

The father said, "It doesn't work like that. He doesn't need another cookie."

The yellow pantsuit lady had rested her hands on the son's shoulders and shook her spidery gray curls. She told the father that it wasn't up to him. She'd said, "Nobody's asking you."

On this trip to the grocery store, the father gave the daughter a roll of quarters and left her in front of the giant claw machine. "Good luck," he told her. He strapped the son in the cart. Bread, milk, eggs, cheese. *Get whatever makes sense*, the mother said. *It isn't brain surgery.*

One hundred and seventeen smoke-free days, and the rubber band was still around the father's wrist. The son pulled a twig out of his pocket and slid it under the father's rubber band, then a popsicle stick, then his own wet bony finger. "Don't even think about it," the father warned.

Last time, when they got home, the mother looked as though she'd been crying. The father touched the telephone in the kitchen – the receiver felt hot. There were dirty dishes in one side of the kitchen sink and there were ashes in the other. The mother didn't come out to the car and help unload the bags; instead, she locked herself in the bathroom. The son had piled all of his favorite toys – his garbage truck and dump truck, his front end loader and log skidder – in front of the bathroom door. It wasn't until he tried to shove a half-eaten cookie under the door that the mother would come out.

It had made the father wonder: should he be happy because she and her lover were fighting? Or should he be unhappy because the mother was obviously miserable about it?

It was hard to know.

As they stood in line to pay for the groceries, the father hoped that the mother wasn't at home crying. He slipped the leather cover off the checkbook and tossed it on the bottom rack of the cart. The father was writing out a check and he was hoping that if she was crying, she wouldn't want him to ask what was wrong, and if he couldn't resist asking, he hoped she wouldn't tell him.

The son's motor noises softened into an idle; he was eyeballing the name tag pinned to the check-out girl's smock. *Hi! I'm Cathy*, it said. There was a blue ribbon glued to her tag. It said, *Employee of the Month*. The check-out girl was young and blond and plain and pregnant. She said, "Paper or plastic?"

The son lunged for the check-out girl's name tag, but the strap around his waist kept him attached to the cart. The son pinched the father's rubber band between his thumb and index finger and he grinned. "Don't you dare," said the father.

The check-out girl said, "You can have this, sweetheart," and she took off the tag. "But you have to promise to be nice to Daddy. Do you promise?"

"Sure," agreed the son.

Now the check-out girl was grinning. The swell in her belly shifted under her smock.

The daughter was no longer in front of the giant claw machine. She was standing in front of a video game. There was a wobbly stack of quarters on top of the control panel and the empty quarter roll paper was on the floor. There was a teenage boy pounding on buttons and jerking levers. "You were wrong, Dad," the daughter said. She clutched a stuffed pink pig. "He says you just have to know what you're doing. You have to know how to maneuver the claw just right."

The boy briefly glanced up. He didn't respond to the daughter's praise. The father thought he seemed normal enough – just another kid in blue jeans and a tee-shirt, sneakers and a baseball cap – but something was off. Something was strange and wrong. "Let's go," he told the daughter.

"Call me," she told the boy.

In the car, driving home, the father figured it out: eyeliner. The boy had been wearing black eyeliner. And the son, in his car seat, was wearing a name tag that said, *Hi! I'm Cathy*. And there was the daughter, in the passenger seat, arms folded across her chest, pink pig on her lap; she was staring out the window, lost in her thoughts as she stroked her nipples through her

shirt. In the house, there were dirty dishes in the kitchen sink and there was a teacup with two smashed butts on the kitchen table. The kitchen receiver was cold, but the mother was smiling. Hanging next to the scissors around her neck, there was a gold charm shaped like a hair dryer.

At the airplane parts factory, there were layoffs, and the father's job was one of five hundred

Many Will Enter, Few Will Win

cut. On his first unemployed morning, he sat at the kitchen table while the mother scrambled eggs and fried potatoes, and the son drank orange juice and kicked the daughter under the table. The daughter kicked him back, then returned to her homework. She was alphabetizing state capitals.

The father took off his rubber band and aimed it at the ceiling, the trash bin, the window. He aimed it at the collection of gold-plated spoons hanging on the wall in the hallway, then at the mother's backside. "Cigarettes," he said.

"Yes," said the son.

"You're so oral, Daddy," the daughter said. She dipped her pencil eraser in a puddle of ketchup. She stuck the lead tip of it in her mouth, and while staring directly at him, she inhaled, then exhaled.

The rubber band hit the back of the mother's thigh, just below where her nightgown ended. A red mark appeared. The mother didn't stop scrambling eggs to rub her thigh; she didn't stop frying potatoes. She didn't turn to look at the father, but the children did. "It was an accident," he said. "I didn't mean for it to happen. I didn't hurt her."

"Okay," said the son. The rubber band was on the floor in front of the stove. He picked it up and ran away.

"Don't look so worried," the father said.

"Who's worried?" said the daughter. Her fringed bangs hung over her eyes. She was wearing a baseball cap and lots of black eyeliner. When the father started smoking again, it was a relief.

At first, he only smoked with his morning coffee. Before long, he added a cigarette after supper, then another one at bedtime. He lit cigarettes off the stove, and he used a teacup for an ashtray, the toilet bowl, the kitchen sink. The hair on his wrists grew back, thick and blond. By the time his unemployment checks ran out, the father was back to more than a pack a day. His moustache stank, but he could shave his moustache.

In the basement beauty shop, the father sat on the swivel chair. He was tapping ashes into the brass box the mother kept her business cards in. She stood over him, lathering his face with shaving cream. When she was pregnant with the son, she'd asked the father to shave her legs. She'd been sitting on the toilet seat, wearing his briefs. *You're staring at me like you've never seen me before*, she said. *What is your problem?* and he'd said he didn't know. Now she was resting one hand on top of his head and she was shaving off his moustache in short, even strokes. His bald upper lip made him look forlorn. The skin was as smooth as a girl's. When he tried to kiss the mother on the mouth, she turned her face.

The girl behind the counter at the doughnut shop was young and blond and plain and grossly pregnant. She was wearing a pin that said, *Be Patient With Me. I'm New.* She pretended not to notice when the father slipped an aluminum ashtray in his pocket. She pretended not to hear the old man sitting beside him at the counter say, "What

Many Will Enter, Few Will Win

kind of bee makes milk?" The doughnut girl stood with her feet wide apart. She was resting her hands on top of her belly. She was grinning at the father. "I know you," she said.

"I don't think so," said the father.

"A booby," said the old man.

The mother wouldn't let the father stay at home much during the day. She said she had a business to run and while the children were gone – junior high and nursery school – he needed to keep himself busy. He needed a job, a hobby, *something*. Something besides sitting in her beauty shop on the swivel chair gawking at the clients. The mother said he made the clients uncomfortable. They were women with curlers in their hair and mud masks on their faces. They were P.T.A. moms and single mothers and grandmas. They were old ladies and high school girls and bridal parties. They were breasts and wombs and menstrual cycles. Both times the mother was pregnant, she'd weighed more than he did. The doughnut girl looked like she weighed more, too.

"Pregnant gals have nice boobies," the old man said. "Big. Like hers." He jutted his chin toward the doughnut girl. He had flabby little boobies sticking out under his shirt. He was elbowing the father. "Don't they?"

The father lit a cigarette and said he didn't know.

He was wondering: what is pregnancy? You spend a few moments inside her and then she becomes somebody's mother. What the old man said might be true, but was it right to say so? Was it even something that should be noticed? He had knelt between the mother's knees, the hair on her legs coarse and dark, and he'd squirted a line of shaving cream down her calf. It was summer and she was pregnant with the son. The mother had her hair clipped back off her neck. This was before she wore the long necklace with the gold charms. Her due date had passed and her doctor said that making love was something she and the father could do to get labor started.

He was thinking that if he pushed open the door to a motel room, maybe he'd find her there, naked, and her lover there, too, also naked. Maybe they're just getting started or maybe they're just finishing because he couldn't see them doing anything, but laying there naked across the bed, eyes closed, shoulder touching shoulder, hip touching hip, each of them pressing the sole of a foot against the other's.

"Are you sure I don't know you?" said the doughnut girl.

"I think she wants a date," said the old man. "I think she likes you."

"You don't know me," said the father.

It won't work, he'd told the mother. He was on his knees, looking up over the belly, lined with stretch marks and no longer taut, past the breasts, heavy and large and no longer firm, up the neck, the double chin, to her mouth. She was frowning. She said she wanted to make love. She said she was

Many Will Enter, Few Will Win

miserable. She wanted to get this pregnancy over with. She said, *How do you know it won't work?*

His arms wouldn't fit around her. Her skin was papery and dry. Her lips were cracked. The bulge in her belly shifted. She looked terrible; the father couldn't even kiss her. The bathroom wasn't big enough for both of them, and the daughter was pounding on the other side of the door, and he said, *I won't do it. It's not going to work, honey. And I'm afraid of hurting you.*

In the doughnut shop, there was a dark, wet stain in the crotch of the old man's trousers and the smell of urine. There was powdered sugar on his lips and his eyes were closed, like he was sleeping.

There was a cigarette burning in an ashtray; the doughnut girl waved away the smoke. The father looked at her closely. There was a wedding ring on her finger and the swell under her smock pushed against the counter. Both of her hands were pressing against the small of her back. Her hair was pulled back from her face and stuffed under a cap. He saw in the motel room, the lover kissing the mother's hip, her stomach, her shoulder. The lover kissing the mother on the mouth. The father rose, ever-so-slightly, and stretched across the counter to press his lips against the doughnut girl's. "You know me," the father whispered. "You've seen me before."

The palm of her hand smacked hard across his cheek. "What is the matter with you?" she said.

When the father got home, the mother wasn't there. He asked where she was, and the daughter said she didn't know. He asked when she'd be back, and the daughter said she really didn't know. Then the father went in the bathroom. The son piled his toys in front of the door, but the father didn't come out. He was in there for a long time.

The daughter had a secret: she hadn't gone to school. She'd played hooky with the boy who wore black eyeliner. She knew about penises, but she'd never given much thought to testicles. The boy's testicles were interesting – two little balls hanging loosely in a wrinkled sack, like an afterthought, between his legs. As soon as she touched them, the boy groaned like she'd hurt him. His eyes got teary and the eyeliner smudged. *See what you did?* he'd said. *Now it's too late.*

When the father finally came out of the bathroom, the mother still wasn't home. He tripped over the son's dump truck and stepped on the name tag that read, *Hi! I'm Cathy.* The sole of the father's foot was tender and pale, and the pin went in deep. Instead of pulling it out, he hobbled to the kitchen to show the children.

The daughter was slicing a banana, and she was tossing chunks of it toward the son's open mouth. She was teaching him how to tell his left from his right. Every time the son caught the banana, he had to pull his hair with his left hand. Every time he missed, he had to pull it with his right. He kept getting mixed up. "You'll learn," said the daughter. When he saw the name tag sticking out of the father's foot, he yanked it out and ran away.

The daughter bent over to look more closely at the father's foot. There was a small hole in the meaty part of it, and there was a drop of blood coming out of the hole. She pressed her thumb against the hole. She said, "Are you going to be all right?"

"Maybe," he said. "I think so," but his foot still throbbed.

If I Close Them

Knowing his name, Casey said, was my first mistake.

His name was Taylor, and convincing him to come with us didn't take much imagination: a ride in air-conditioning, the promise of an ice cream. A few weeks before, I'd buzzed off his hair. A crew cut, I told him, was just the right look for a little boy. Casey rubbed her hand across the top of his head and said he looked like a soldier. Taylor liked that. Sun had bleached his hair and hatched freckles across his nose. His eyes were brown. He was thin, small for his age. I wasn't his mother, but I loved him.

That, Casey said, was my second mistake.

Taylor was related to her by patchwork, her sister Dana's step-son. We threw his bike in the bed of the truck, where Reggie sat, panting, her tail thumping against the spare, and we put Taylor in the space between us. This time, it was his face, a bruise on his cheek, purple, turning yellow, noticeable even under a layer of make-up. There was a deep cut in the center of it, Dana's ring, its sharp stone.

Casey was driving, so I strapped the seat belt around him. She was gentle with most things: pulling a splinter out of Reggie's paw, burrs from her tail and ears, brushing tangles out of her coat. Casey was thirty-one, seven years older than me, lines around her eyes and mouth from being outdoors. Her hair was long and dark blonde, and she wore it twisted in a single thick braid. She was wide-hipped, narrow-waisted, tall. Casey was beautiful. When she stuck her hand in our aquarium, the fish rose to the surface to kiss her fingers. When we went fishing, she wet her hands before taking a trout off a hook and throwing it back. She'd watch a movie before I did so she could tell me which parts I'd want to turn away from.

But Casey was a reckless driver. Too fast, too confident. The back roads of western Pennsylvania are narrow and winding, made shady by dense brush and thick trees, woods that deer spring out of four and five at a time. Sometimes, Casey would loop around those roads with her hat pulled down low, covering her face, just to show me she could.

"You're peeking through the mesh," I'd tell her.

"Never," she'd say.

I was pregnant with my second, a girl Jay would name Georgia after his grandmother, but we didn't know this at the time. I wouldn't know for another month, and by that time, Casey and I had broken up.

More than once Casey said to me, "I can't trust you, Samantha. I won't put my heart into something you're only curious about."

She was right to be afraid. I never would have described myself as a lesbian – the word sounded bitter, like a mouthful of pennies – but I wasn't ever able to describe what it was I felt about Casey, either. My feelings were something I swerved around with my eyes closed.

I lied to her. I didn't tell her the reason the power went out was because I'd been too dreamy to get the check out on time, ignoring the first overdue notice and forgetting about the second. I told her I'd gone out to pick blackberries, but not that I hadn't been alone. When she noticed how quickly we ran out of green tea, I said I drank a lot, a pot a day, never mentioning Jay's mug. I glossed over how often Taylor came by. Casey and I had been living together since January, and in June, I still wouldn't tell her when my mother called – long distance from Shaker Heights – because then I'd have to admit that, yes, I'd mentioned her, but only in passing, and only as my roommate.

That summer, the transmission in my car finally gave out, so we only had Casey's truck, a stick shift I couldn't drive. I was a few credits shy of my teaching degree; classes ended in early May, and without a place to go or a way to get there, I spent my mornings waiting for Taylor to ride his bike – almost two miles from Dana's place – to the farmhouse we rented. While Casey worked at the animal shelter, I'd pour glasses of chocolate milk topped with whipped cream. I fried sausage patties and baked coffee cake with cinnamon butter and blackberry jam.

Casey wouldn't eat any of it. "Poisoning yourself," she said. No meat, no sugar, no dairy, she didn't even put dressing on her salad. She steamed broccoli and kale and she'd eat it out of the pan while standing over the sink.

I was waiting for Taylor to show up, stand outside the kitchen window, straddling his bike, until I noticed him and let him in. On certain days – especially Saturday and Sunday mornings – there'd be scratches on his arms and neck. Or his nose would be swollen. Or his eye, black. On the fifth of July, when his arm was in a sling, and he found out he could ride his bike no-hands if he had to, I said I was calling Children's Services.

"I'll talk to Dana," Casey promised. "She's just young."

"She's older than me," I said.

"She drinks too much."

"That's an excuse?"

"No," Casey said, "but she's my sister and I said I'd talk to her. I don't see why it ever needs to go beyond that." She paused. Despite living just a few miles from her, Casey didn't see a lot of Dana. I'd met her only twice. She was a thin, twitchy woman with circles the color of eggplant under her eyes. One time, she wanted to borrow Casey's truck; the other, she wanted to borrow fifty dollars. Both times, Casey gave her what she wanted. Right now, Casey was saying, "Doesn't that kid have any friends his own age?"

I shrugged.

She said, "He's not yours."

I told her I already knew that, and she said of course I did. She hooked a strand of hair behind my ear and told me not to think about it. She told me I didn't have to think about anything at all.

Casey wasn't wild about children. They were loud and demanding. They were the gum stuck to the bottom of her running shoes. They were the popsicle stick she hit while roller blading, a scar on her elbow. "I'd rather be a dog mother," she said.

There was another scar, round and deep, the size of a cigarette, on her shoulder. That first night, I touched it, this mystery, on a body like my own. "My grandmother," she said. "She raised Dana and me. We were wild kids. Gave her fits. But we never got anything we didn't deserve."

"You think you deserved this?"

"It got my attention," Casey said. "Dana, though. She was a hardhead, got knocked around even worse. She survived. We both did."

"My mother never put a hand on me."

"Lucky you," Casey said.

If I Close Them

I put my hand on her face, her neck, her hip. She put her fingers across my mouth.

I didn't push Taylor to talk about what went on at home. Imagining it came easy enough. I'd seen the couple who adopted my son only once: the woman's hands pressed against the nursery window; the man's hands on her shoulders. I saw those hands as claws. Turning them into fists came too easily. I don't let myself imagine what doesn't seem possible.

I'd fuss over Taylor and he let me. When I pulled him on my lap, he tensed, squirmed, trying to wiggle away. But I wouldn't let him go, rocking until I felt his body relax.

We talked. I told him I was going to be a teacher, and he said he hoped I'd be a nice one. I told him Reggie had been a stray Casey found in the woods, starved-skinny and skittish, trying to nurse three dead pups. "Something to break your heart," she said.

Taylor told me his real mother was in Michigan and that Dana put too much mustard in his tuna sandwiches. He said Dana told him Casey and I were dykes. "Whatever *that* is," he said. He said he wanted to join the Marines, like his dad, so he could be stationed in Italy, too. "Pow! Pow!" he shouted, and he'd aim his finger at me, aim a stick, the garden hose. He once bit a piece of toast into the shape of a gun. One time, Jay tickled him until he collapsed, very dramatically, to the ground, curling up his legs, shielding his face with his arms. When Jay bent down and tapped his shoulder, Taylor's fist shot out, struck Jay's neck.

"I didn't mean to," Taylor said. He had a strange way of smiling when he thought he was in trouble. Forced. Looking not at you, but over you. "I didn't mean it."

"You're strong," Jay said.

"That wasn't nice, little kid," I told him.

Taylor, still smiling, said, "Do you hate me now?"

At first, Jay came around the farmhouse because Reggie had been shot. He was a veterinarian, working mostly on large animals, making calls to dairy farms and horse barns, but he knew Casey from the shelter, and told her he'd stop by and check on her dog. We let Reggie run loose, and people knew her, recognized her floppy spotted ears and freckled coat, paws the size of small melons.

"Your dog is a thief, Casey," John Klaus said. He'd caught Reggie dragging away the antlers he'd tacked to his shed. "Next time I won't tell you first."

Reggie chased deer into his cornfield. She brought home the broom Old Lady McMullen kept propped against her back door, Mrs. Charter's welcome mat, one of Chuck Monroe's work boots. She carried home a litter of kittens, one at a time, and hid them under our front porch.

"You're a problem child," Casey said, rubbing Reggie's neck, that place under her collar. "You better be good. I don't want to tie you."

If I Close Them

Casey was positive Reggie had been hit by some fraternity guys from the college, the ones who spotted deer illegally. She suspected they were the ones who, that spring, had killed the fawn. In June, Casey and I had run into them at My Brother's Place, the local watering hole, where the tall red-haired guy staggered over to our booth. "Which is the man?" he said.

Casey ignored him, drank her beer, but in bed that night she turned away from me. "I wish people would mind their own business," she said.

"It's a small town." I ran my hand down the length of her back, which was long and narrow, unblemished. I reached over her shoulder to smooth my finger across her scar.

She inched away. "Is there enough room on your side?" she said.

"Forget about that jerk."

"You didn't grow up here."

"I don't care what people think."

Casey said, "Why don't you tell your mother that?" She slipped out of bed and went to the living room, turned on the television, Reggie padding after her.

I warned Taylor about how he handled the kittens. I'd caught him swinging one around by its hind legs. He thought it was funny to watch it walk dizzily, trying to regain its balance. When Casey saw him do it, she yelled, startling him; he flinched and jumped on his bike, didn't come back for a week. When Casey found the calico, neck broken, at the end of the lane, she buried it and didn't say anything. I figured she blamed one of the neighbor's dogs – it seemed possible, and it's what I decided to believe.

During the first week of August, I made the mistake of telling Casey something my mother had said. My mother had gone to a wedding in Cleveland. "The colors were white and black," my mother said, "and so were the bride and groom."

Casey said my mother was a racist. "Disguising it with cleverness." It had rained that morning, and gray clouds swirled around the sky, threatening to rain again. We were stringing a wire between two trees to make a dog run. The night before Reggie destroyed Mrs. Charter's lawn ornaments – Little Bo Peep and two of her sheep. Bo's checkered dress and blue bonnet were torn to shreds, her wooden head gouged with teeth marks. Reggie left her in Mrs. Charter's driveway. The sheep fared better: we found one in a ditch and the other under our porch.

John Klaus had called before sunrise. "That's it, Casey," he warned. "Tie your dog up or bury her."

"You don't even know my mother," I said.

"I don't have to. She'd hate me."

My baby's father had offered to marry me, but my mother talked me out of it. I was a senior in high school. "You want a life," she said, "not a husband who has braces on his teeth." My father died when I was twelve, old enough for my mother to take back some life of her own. She left me alone a lot; I watched television and ate bowls of cereal. "My mother hates anyone I'm dating," I said. "That doesn't make her a horrible person."

"What does that make her?"

"A mother."

"Lucky you," said Casey.

Catching Reggie wasn't easy; she was hiding deep under the porch. Casey whistled and called for her. Poured food in her dish. She even crawled under the porch with a ball of hamburger. But Reggie just whined and inched further back.

"She knows she's in trouble," I said.

"Fuck John Klaus," Casey said. "I'm leaving her loose." She sat beside me on the front step and clipped the ends of the chain together. "That kitten," she said. She was looking at the ground. "I don't want Taylor coming around here so much. I'm telling Dana to keep him home."

"I wouldn't—"

She cut me off. "Dana has a temper and maybe she shouldn't be whaling on him as much as she does, but I don't see how that's our problem. He's not even her kid." She put her arm around me, the skin on the underside of her wrist soft against my shoulder. "I only want you," she said. "What do you want?"

Whatever Jay knew or wondered or thought about Casey and me, he kept to himself. He was stocky and strong. He had a moustache and a beard that was just starting to gray, but there was hardly any hair on his arms. "I'm highly evolved," he said.

Long sleeves protected my arms from thorny bushes heavy with blackberries. I promised Taylor I'd bake him a pie if he put the berries in the bucket instead of smashing them in his fist. I told Jay he needed to loop his belt through his bucket's handle so he could use both hands for picking. He pretended he didn't understand. "Fix it for me?" he said.

I did. Unbuckled his belt. Pulled out the strap. Then Taylor shot between us. He crashed into Jay who scooped him up and tossed him in the air. Reggie barked. The morning sun moved higher; the sky went hazy. Taylor wrapped his legs around Jay's waist and Jay skimmed his head across Taylor's crew cut. "Feels like a monkey's butt," he said.

Taylor said, "Do you wish you had a boy like me?"

I saw a table set, three plates, cloth napkins, polished silver. I wanted to cook an enormous meal – a ham, a roast, stuff a turkey, casseroles and potatoes, salads and pies, food we'd be eating for days. I saw the wet dark hair and scrunched-up face of the boy I'd held for half an hour.

That was what I wanted.

There was no way to tell Casey.

Taylor's hands and face and white tee-shirt were purple-sticky, and he was demanding that

Reggie "Sit! Speak!" before he tossed her another berry.

"You're a mess, little kid," I told him.

"I am?"

"You are."

Taylor stood very still for a moment, then he threw himself on the ground, knees to chest, hands over his face. "Dana," he said. His voice was muffled. "She said don't get dirty."

Jay and I looked at each other. Jay said, "This isn't a big deal." Reggie was licking Taylor's leg; he kicked at her. "Or is it?"

"That shirt's stained. I can wash it, but it'll never come clean."

"Taylor," Jay said, "let's go to K-Mart. Let's go get you a clean shirt."

There was no way to tell Casey.

Not about Taylor changing clothes in the parking lot, how I tugged the shirt over his head, telling him, "Raise your arms. Skin the bunny," which was something my mother used to say to me while the bathtub filled. When I closed my eyes, I could see Casey as a little girl, wiry and blonde, a cigarette pressing against her shoulder, but I couldn't tell her about the marks I saw on Taylor's stomach and back, bruises the shape of fingerprints on his shoulders. I put my lips against them while Jay felt his bones. We drove Taylor back to the farmhouse and put him on his bike, watched him ride away. No need to warn him, "Don't tell."

There was no way to tell Casey about Jay and me, returning to the blackberry bushes to gather our buckets. We held hands, then he kissed me and I wanted him to. The grassy clearing was itchy, but not unpleasant, his legs entwined with mine, the humid air, the hazy sky, our bodies slick. I kept my eyes opened and looked at his face because if I closed them, I'd see Casey.

After Jay left, I put Reggie on the dog run. It was a four mile walk to the animal shelter and I didn't want her following me. All the way there, I had this idea about how I could get my hands on Taylor, how I could keep him, not let him go back to Dana's. Call Dana up and tell her I'd be taking him or else turning her in to Children's Services. It seemed possible she wouldn't put up a fight. I let myself forget he had a mother in Michigan and a father in Italy. I saw myself standing outside the dressing room while Taylor tried on school clothes. I saw myself teaching him spelling and long division, going to soccer games and Cub Scout meetings, visiting my mother, *Here is your grandson.* I saw myself tucking Taylor in at night, but my mind refused to put Casey cheering in the stands or standing in his bedroom beside me.

As soon as I hit the parking lot, I could heard the noise of barking dogs. "You walked?" Casey said. "In this heat? You must miss me." She was hosing out empty cages, her hair tucked up under her hat, her arms and legs tan and strong. She smiled at me, the same way she had when I held a new blouse against my chest, asking if she liked it. She'd nodded, wide-eyed, stroking the neckline, smiling.

If I Close Them

I stuck around the shelter, helping Casey feed the animals, agreeing we should think about taking in one of those black and tan border collie mix pups. "Reggie might get jealous," Casey said, "but she'd survive. It'd be fun to raise a puppy."

Later, when we pulled in the driveway, there was Reggie, attached to the dog run, jumping up and down, thrilled to see us, struggling against the chain, choking on her collar. "Who tied up my dog?" Casey said. "Somebody tied her and didn't leave her any water."

I shrugged. I never thought about filling her bowl.

"Klaus, that asshole," Casey said.

There was Taylor, hiding behind a tree, the bruise on his cheek covered with make-up. Casey licked her thumb, then wiped at it. "Did you fall down?" she said.

He nodded.

Casey said, "We're going to take you home, Taylor, and I'm going to talk to Dana about ways to help you be more careful."

I met Casey at a Christmas party at my art professor's house. I was wearing a button pin that had the letter "L" with a slash through it. Noel. One of the kids at the kindergarten where I did my student teaching gave it to me, and I thought it was cute. But a woman at the party, a little drunk, a little stoned, thought the button meant "No Lesbians," and was giving me all sorts of grief about it.

Casey thought this was hilarious, especially since I didn't know – couldn't tell – the woman was herself a lesbian. Later, Casey would ask, "How could you not know?" and I'd say, "Why should I care?"

"You are what you love," Casey said.

That's where she's mistaken: it's not what you love, but who, and how.

Convincing Casey to drive into town for ice cream before taking Taylor home wasn't too difficult: a little boy with a splotch of make-up on his face; a woman who couldn't stop touching him, stroking his cheek, squeezing his shoulders. Taylor said, "I like ice cream."

I said, "Me, too."

"I hate ice cream," said Casey, "but since Samantha wants some, I guess we have to."

We had Taylor in the truck, Reggie in the back, her ears perked up, her nose sniffing at something in the wind. Casey was taking the long way into town, dirt roads. She put her arm across the back of the seat and fluffed up my hair. There was no way to tell her about Jay and me except to come out and say it, which I didn't, not ever. There wasn't reason or opportunity to: even though Casey would to talk Dana – again – and even though Dana would make promises – again – I still made the call, and a few days later, a social worker would visit.

Casey would say, "Did you get what you wanted?"

She'd say, "You went behind my back."

She'd say, "I don't see that this is working

If I Close Them

out between us."

But right now, in her truck, Casey was picking up speed, curving around a winding road. "Dana's going to wonder where you are," she was saying to Taylor. "You looking for trouble?"

"No."

"You trying to make her mad?"

"No."

"Are you going to be good, stay out of her way?"

"He's good," I said.

"I'm good," Taylor said.

The sky was turning darker, the evening going softer, still warm, and we were headed around a bend. "Watch this, Taylor," Casey said. She revved the engine. Pulled her hat down low. Her eyes closed, she never saw the deer, but somehow, she managed to miss it.

What Remains

There once was a boy in a Pittsburgh Pirates cap, a logger who left twenty percent even when the waitress was surly and the food, cold. He sat in my section, day after day, lunch after lunch, ordering the same thing every time.

"A cheeseburger with lettuce and mayonnaise, please," my granddaughter recites. Reva has been hearing me tell this story since she was a girl who wrapped a dish towel around her hair like a princess' turban, who pretended the potato masher balancing on her head was a tiara. She's a grown woman now – or at least what passes for one these days – and her everafter includes an estranged husband to whom she won't speak, though he's called several times, as well as a child. You'd think she'd be tired of fairy tales.

Or maybe she's just humoring me. Reva has not been forthcoming with details regarding her situation, and I only know what her mother has passed along. Reva left Marc, Gloria reported. There is no other woman. He's never hit her. He's good with the baby, fixing bottles and changing diapers. He hands over his signed paycheck every Friday. What else, Gloria puzzled, could the girl possibly want?

Well, there's plenty of what else to want, and if my former daughter-in-law doesn't know that by now, I am not going to be the one who educates her. Gloria was never impressed with the job I did raising her husband; she thinks I passed my lack of morals onto Dennis, along with his red hair and sweet tooth. Because she might not be entirely wrong, I won't speak poorly of her. Instead, I am going to be happy that my granddaughter has chosen to be here, in my house, sitting at my kitchen table, listening to me rattle on.

But for how long? Reva has been here for less than a week, and while I wish she'd drink the milk left in the bottom of her cereal bowl instead of dumping it down the drain, I'm not in a big hurry for her to leave any time soon. But Reva insists this is only a visit, not a solution.

I also wish she's rinse out the sink after she's brushed her teeth.

It's not vain, I tell her, to say I was something pretty to look at when I was young, small-boned and thin, but curvy, nonetheless, a thick auburn braid hanging past my waist. My cheekbones then and now are high and wide, but since I've reached a certain age, my skin tightening in some places and going slack in others, those bones in my face have become more prominent, like that alien a few years back that wanted to phone home.

Don't think my students didn't notice: they made the resemblance known.

But as a girl, I drew plenty of male attention, more than my fair share, like I was a yellow light they didn't want to speed through. Farmers and salesmen, young boys and old men, I was never silly about their attention, not like those girls who think acknowledging a man's attention breeds more attention. Oh, it does, but the wrong kind. Ignoring a man: that's what makes him crazy with wanting you.

"You mean playing hard to get," Reva says.

"Yes," I tell her. "That's precisely what I mean."

"Well," Reva says, "I'm glad women today are free from that kind of false modesty. These days a woman can ask and she shall receive." She winks. "At least that's what I always do."

I ignore this because that's what Reva wants from me, her ridiculous old grandmother who is a prig and a prude. She's sharp, though. When the girl was eleven, she needed reminding to wash her hair and Q-tip her ears, but she could still see that her parents were a mess: her mother spending more time at Ladies' Bible Study than at home; her father pursuing newer interests all the time – other women, of course – my Dennis has been married four times himself, so it's fair to say Reva probably learned all about what-else-is-there from him. But he also went off to fly fishing clinics and took lessons on how to play the tenor banjo, learned how to set up and maintain saltwater aquariums, and

What Remains

then studied up on organic gardening. Dennis is one to go, go, go. I admire that quality. Dennis is my youngest child as well as my favorite. Most recently, he went through an agility training course with Bobby, a dog he no longer likes or wants and so passed off to Reva. Now Bobby has come to stay with me, along with Reva and her baby. I'm afraid I've fallen in love with him: Bobby will be my last, my it, for dogs and my love.

Not because I've grown cynical with old age, but more because I can't stand the looks of them, the old men – their ears and noses growing hair and getting bigger still, their bumpy arms and lips the color and texture of raw liver. I wouldn't put liver to my mouth as a girl, and I am certainly not about to do so now.

I wasn't a stupid girl, I tell Reva. I wasn't naïve. I could see the boy in the Pittsburgh Pirates cap was unaccustomed to any woman disregarding him. Those green eyes! That polite charm! And me, twenty-one years old, working at the diner while I went to Normal School. This was during wartime, and for Reva, I make myself sound like a young, adventurous, available co-ed, working hard for family and country – for her, I censor. The truth is I was already three years married to Reva's grandfather, who at this time was fighting in France; I was already mother to two babies.

But still, that other boy persisted, until he made sure to get my attention, one day catching me off guard by changing his order. "A cheeseburger with lettuce and mayonnaise, please," he said, "and

I'll also have the meatloaf special and a chocolate shake, scrambled eggs with country toast, pancakes, and an order of fries, a chicken fried steak, mashed potatoes, and a slice of peach pie, as long as it's fresh today. Is it fresh today?" he said, putting unnecessary emphasis on the word "fresh."

It's true, I tell Reva. I was amused enough to play his game, so I brought him all he asked for, and I served it to him, but I did not let on how he'd flattered me. I conducted myself appropriately, and I did not return his smile. I sat on a stool at the counter, smoking a cigarette while I watched him eat. Oh, it took him the better part of an afternoon! It's not like he was some big fat man – his hips were narrow, his belly, flat, but he had strong arms and wide hands, clean fingernails despite his work outdoors. It charmed me to know he went elsewhere to scrub his hands before coming to the diner.

After a while, he wasn't smiling, either, but he choked it all down, and he held it down, until he stood up, making a face like he was going to throw up, which he did, in the trash bin behind the counter where we scraped the plates. He didn't ask for it, but I brought him a glass of water anyway.

"You've made your point," I told him.

"You pity me," he said. "That's a start."

So I fell in love, I tell my granddaughter. End of story.

Reva applauds. "That's what I want," she says. "A romance like you and Grandpa Wayne." Reva has always been the only one to appreciate this story, and in all the times I've told it, I never confessed that the boy in the Pittsburgh Pirates cap is not her grandfather.

Lately, though, I've wanted to. I would like her to know that I know what it is like to get used to your husband, predicting his reactions, learning his moods and behaviors until there is nothing left that's new to learn. There is comfort in that, but no excitement. Had Reva's grandfather been alive, he would have said that Marc, her husband, is not the liveliest fish in the tank – the closest Wayne ever came to calling a person simple. Wayne passed away when Reva was just a baby, heart failure, and it never would have occurred to him that she would someday grow up to have an affair.

Reva has yet to lose the twenty-five pounds she gained during her pregnancy, but you can still see the Homecoming Queen she used to be: a thick rope of pale yellow hair, freckles sprinkled across her nose, two thousand dollars worth of payment plan orthodontics. I treasure the girl, but her infidelity is something I am certain of, the way other women can tell you a cake's recipe with just one taste.

Of course, she denies it.

"Sure, Grandma, I'm screwing the boys who come through my lunch line," she says, smart-alecky because the cafeteria where she works is John F. Kennedy Elementary, where I taught third grade until retirement. I swatted her father's behind for giving me an eighth of that kind of sass, but my granddaughter was raised by people who didn't believe in spanking children. What was it Gloria wanted me to say? Oh, yes: "Use your words, please, sweetheart." Right now, Reva's words include the kind of foul language you used to hear only vulgar men say around other vulgar men. "I'm fucking countless boys in between potty training my two-year-old and bleaching dirty socks."

Her husband called again this morning, and Reva announced, "I'm not here," loudly, so the boy couldn't help but hear her. "She's killing me, Mrs. Clancy," he said to me, and I felt no small amount of pity for him. Wayne would not be wrong: Marc is rather simple, but he's sweet, too. Early in their courtship, both of them still babies themselves, high school seniors, Reva already pregnant, she brought Marc over to meet me, and I watched him pick up her fingernail clippings (I really wish she wouldn't trim her fingernails at the kitchen table) and arrange them into the shape of a heart.

"You have a husband who loves you," I tell her. I'm testing the waters here, curious about what she'll say.

She says, "Depending on who's defining it, don't I wish." Frankly, I don't believe her.

Neither does Bobby-the-dog, who is a handsome fellow, half Border Collie, half German Shepard, smarter than your average third grader, stubborn as a brick. Every morning, Bobby and I follow a routine: while we wait for the coffee to drip, he sits at my feet, watching me slather peanut

What Remains

butter across a slice of bread. Bobby's cupcake, we call it. We have to do this covertly, before Reva and the baby get up, as my granddaughter believes the dog has allergies – to dog foods made from corn products, to dust motes and rag weed, to other dogs and to his own hair. He's itchy all the time, she points out, and he is constantly scratching, so she buys him expensive kibbles, which, in the two weeks Bobby has been here now, secretly feasting on cupcakes, he's come to reject. It puzzles the girl.

Sometimes, I say the word in casual conversation, as in "I have a craving for a chocolate cupcake; why don't you scoot over to the bakery?" or "How's your father and his latest cupcake?" just to watch the dog's ears perk up, his throaty whine, his thumping tail, just to see my granddaughter's bewildered expression. "What is his problem?" she says, and I just shrug, innocent.

"For a dog that won't eat, he's getting pretty fat," she says.

"Maybe he's got a problem with his thyroid," I suggest, after waiting as long as I dare to answer her.

"Nothing would be a surprise," she says.

We also go for walks, Bobby and I. There is a golf course attached to Lincoln Park, just blocks from my house here on Main Street, and there's a large fenced-in field where golfers go to practice their swings and where people can let their dogs off the leash. Bobby and I are the first ones there every morning, six o'clock sharp, except when Mr. Habernot, who is a sneaking snake, and his hellhound, who is a black Lab named Zach, get there first.

Otherwise, this walk is a peaceful moment in my day, a legitimate reason to leave the house, strolling through the dewy lush grass, throwing Bobby a stick, then glancing down to find a golf ball, white or yellow, nested in the thick grass like an Easter egg. As long as we're there before Mr. Habernot and Zach, I always stumble across six or eight, and one day, I found twelve. I put the golf balls in my pockets, which are deep – like all elementary school teachers, my dresses have big pockets – to bring home for the baby.

It took having grandchildren to learn what simple fact that as a parent I never considered: you have to be nice to children when they are small and boring if you want them to be nice to you when they evolve into adults with fascinating and complicated lives. After a long day of dealing with other people's children, I didn't have energy or patience left for my own, but Anthony, Reva's son, who is not quite two, thinks I am the most interesting woman in the world. I've asked him about it, and he's said as much. It's because I've trained him that way, of course, and it is also because of the golf balls. Mr. Habernot is my primary competition for them, and he only collects them to sell back to the golfers! But when I give one to Anthony, well, he's appreciative. Tufts of wispy hair sticking straight up, his round red lips puckered around a white golf ball, that baby looks just as innocent and unconcerned as his grandfather, eating pickled eggs, one right after another, until I thought I'd vomit, though I never did.

Why did I fall in love with the boy in the Pittsburgh Pirates cap?

It was the little things he gave me, I tell my granddaughter. It's past two a.m., and the girl is only minutes home, stumbling up the front steps to discover Bobby and me on the porch, waiting for her. Where has she been?

It's not a mystery. Her hair is messy, her blouse is untucked, and there are circles of sweat under her arms, grass stains on the behind of her jeans. She smells like beer and like smoke. Her answers are slurry and vague. "Oh, out and about," she says. "Here, there, and everywhere."

Meaning, it's none of your business, old woman. She's been living with me for a month now, and this is not the only time she's gone out early and come home late. It's not the second time or even the third. But it is the first time I've called it to her attention.

Patting the space beside me, I invite her to sit on the swing. I've got a hot toddy that's mostly bourbon, but it's not something I've been drinking. It's the result of something I remembered about an hour ago, waiting for her. How her father came home inebriated when he was a teenager, and Wayne wasn't fiery and yelling. A showy scene was not ever his way. Instead, Wayne did the hair-of-the-dog trick, serving Dennis a breakfast of

Cheerios and bourbon, then sending him out to mow the lawn. Poor boy! The faces he made tickled Wayne and me both, I must say. We are a family that believes in torturing the ones we love as a way to show how much we love them. I offer Reva a swig of what I've got, but she groans and waves it away, like I knew she would.

"You're going to make me puke, Grandma," she says. "Where's Anthony?"

"Your baby has been sleeping peacefully for hours," I say. "Unlike some people around here."

"Sweet little boy," she says.

I quit smoking when my children were small because of the notes they stuck in my pockets. *Please, Mama, we don't want you to die.* Their father put them up to it, I'm sure, and though I have never appreciated anyone telling me what to do, I quit. Isn't that what love does – bully you, overwhelm you until you are not yourself? What I would give for a menthol cigarette to puff in my granddaughter's direction. I am full of torturous intent when it comes to that girl, but my motives are pure. Meaning, I know a thing or two about where you've been, Missy, as well as where you are, so why not just tell me all about it?

He gave me a raffle ticket, I tell her, that turned out to be worth fifty dollars. He gave me a box trap and a jar of peanut butter that did the trick, snaring the mouse, not killing it, that very same day. We drove that mouse to the country where we let it go. "Your grandfather wrote to me from France," I tell her. "Wayne told me to poison it."

He gave me an animal cracker tin full of antique buttons that had belonged to his mother, who died two weeks before he started coming to the diner for his every meal. When I scooped my hand through buttons made of glass, buttons shaped like flowers and like tears, brass buttons like those on a soldier's uniform, I brought up an enormous yellow tooth.

The tooth, he told me, was the story of his sober mother whacking his drunken father with a cast iron skillet, her attempt to stop his wandering, her way of saying, enough is enough. "It worked, too," I tell Reva. I am not endorsing physical violence, of course, but moments of great passion have always stirred me, like an itch I can't help but scratch.

"What are you saying, Grandma? You want to whack me upside the head with a skillet? Better wait until morning. Right now, I wouldn't feel a thing."

I'd paddle her right now if I could, but Bobby, whose timing is questionable, is suffering from flatulence. "That dog stinks!" Reva says. "Like he's been eating beans or something rotten."

I do not confess that Bobby and I experimented with Mexican food earlier this evening, microwaving the bean burritos we bought at the Seven Eleven. Revealing such would indeed torture Reva, but it would likewise punish me. "Grandma," she's saying, rubbing her eyes, her temples. "What did you mean," she says slowly, "about Grandpa wanted to poison the mouse? Didn't he give you the box trap?"

I've already pointed out that the girl is sharp. Even intoxicated, she doesn't miss a thing, whereas my eagerness to make a point made me careless. "I'm not sure, to what, exactly, you're referring," I tell her. "Did I say something like that?"

"Something like it," she says, but if she's suspicious, she's not pressing further. Reva is stretching, she's yawning, she says she's going to bed. Kissing my cheek, she says, "Thank you, Grandma, for watching Anthony and for worrying about me, and for taking such good care of us. We won't burden you much longer, I promise."

"You're no burden," I say.

"Sweet dreams, Grandma," she says. "I love you."

Don't think I don't know what the girl is up to: keeping us both out of trouble by bringing up the subject of love. What else could be so distracting?

A porch swing can be as comfortable as a bed, and I'm thinking I fell in love with a boy who was not my husband because of how hard he could hit a baseball and how many baseballs he hit just to impress me. Because of how he sat crunched beside me in a booth even when it was just the two of us and I was supposed to be closing up the diner for the night. Because he tried and tried to bully me into doing things I would not do, sexual things, of course, but also things like climbing a tree and running a chainsaw and leaving my husband, and me, receiving a letter that said Wayne would be home in two weeks.

I could tell the girl about all of this, but what would she say? What is your point, Grandma? Are you self-righteous about staying in an unsatisfying marriage or are you full of regrets?

Unlike my granddaughter, who learned to use her words, I don't know how to answer that.

It was not a peaceful night for me, and I wake earlier than usual to take Bobby out. The choke chain gags him, but willful, he pulls on. This is an animal, who instructed to sit, will lower his bottom as close to the floor as he can get it without actually sitting. Instructed to stay, he will scoot himself across the floor, inch by subtle inch, until you notice he is on the other side of the room. These are reasons to love him.

As soon as we reach the golf field, I unclip his leash, and he goes bounding and barking toward Mr. Habernot, the wizened old man in a yellow slicker that I am sure his wife sent him out in, though the sky, while still dark, is quite clear. He's waving at me and waving at me, and Zach, his dog, sits calmly, as Bobby, like a maniac, tears circles around them, barking his fool head off. "Hullo, Mrs. Clancy," Mr. Habernot calls. I can hear the static coming from the geezer's hearing aid well before I reach him. "I guess old Zach and I beat you here this morning."

"I am unaware of any race," I say haughtily.

This is *early* morning, not yet five a.m., and as I step closer, I see Mr. Habernot is looking rather pleased with himself as the pockets on that slicker are bulging with golf balls. Selling them back to the golfers! I cannot imagine. Mr. Habernot retired from the post office; he is far from poor, and he has told me he can get up to a nickel a piece for those golf balls. I feel nothing but pity for his wife for as we all know that a man who is stingy with a dollar is likewise stingy with his heart.

When Wayne came home, I gave up the boy in the Pittsburgh Pirates cap. I suppose I felt guilt at how I'd carried on when he was gone, the sudden freedom I knew, and my mind hooked on to small things he'd done: how, early in our courtship, in a fit of bad temper, I used a hammer to smash a china doll he'd given me, and upon seeing that, those slivers of glass, Wayne didn't return my fury. Instead, he walked out the door, and when he returned, he had another china doll, exactly like the first. How, when he proposed, it was not on bended knee, but on paper, a list of reasons why I should marry him, all of them practical – his ability to provide, his desire to raise a family, own a house. Last on the list was his love for me. How, after we were married, not too long after at all, I didn't need to look at him to know what he was doing: stirring exactly three spoonfuls of sugar into his coffee; looking at his wristwatch at precisely seven o'clock each morning; balancing the checkbook down to the penny; measuring the distance between the front door and the bedroom to calculate how much the new carpeting I wanted but never got would cost.

Mr. Habernot is rummaging through his pockets. "You say your grandson likes these golf balls," he says, "well, you just give him one for me," and he hands me a yellow one, but it's filthy, and dog-chewed, pocked with deep pointy teeth marks. Mr. Habernot grins, like he knows he hasn't done me any favors, and – *Use your words, please, sweetheart!* – I cannot bring myself to thank him.

Instead, I throw that ball as far and as hard as I can, which regrettably, isn't very far or hard, and am mortified when Bobby interferes with my point by fetching it back to me. Stomping off in a huff, though tempting, lacks dignity, so I nod and scratch Bobby's ears as though I think he's a very good dog indeed.

Only half an hour has passed, and I'm back home, in my kitchen, where we're sitting around the table, all of us, Anthony in his high chair, Bobby at my feet. Dogs are true gamblers: sneak Bobby a piece of bacon once and the next ninety-nine times he's willing to bet you'll do it again. I've been telling my granddaughter how sorry I feel for Mr. Habernot's wife. "That bastard!" she says. "She should divorce the S.O.B. She doesn't have to put up with the likes of him."

I sense she's merely placating me. "Tomorrow, you'll have to get there at *four* in the morning," she's saying. "That'll fix him."

"Right around the same time you'll be

getting home," I say. "I won't need to set my alarm."

The girl ignores this. Oh, she's chipper this morning: she's up and showered and letting her hair dry in ringlets around her shoulders. Her skin is clear and her eyes are bright. She's prancing around the kitchen, singing to herself, smiling as she shines the water faucet wipes the counter, sweeps up toast crumbs. She's as happy as those simple-minded women who've discovered an oleo product that has all the taste but half the fat of real butter. Bobby is waiting patiently at my feet, and I am about to sneak him another piece of bacon when Reva, who's been mashing an egg for the baby's breakfast, spins around, waving her fork at me.

"I knew it!" she says. "Tell the truth: you've been feeding bad things to the dog. I'm telling you, Grandma," she says, "don't do that. It's not good for him and you'll make him sick."

Reva is looking at me with one eyebrow raised, a trick that makes her look sly, one that I am certain she inherited from me. I am furious with her, for reasons I suspect, though I hate to admit, have less to do with dogs and bacon and more to do with envy. Because I love the girl, I have decided is to tell my granddaughter the truth, one that she'll won't like hearing, but will have an interest in nonetheless. It's true that I've been feeding the dog bad things, I'll tell her. Peanut butter cupcakes and spicy bean burritos and potato chips and potato salad, bacon and eggs and sweet pickles. Bobby likes sweet pickles. He likes them a lot.

Shared and Stolen

This is about blood in panties: not the blood that means no child, but the blood that means the child is gone. My father says, *You remind me of her – my sister.* He means our high forehead, our pierced ears, the dimples on each side of our mouth. He means the lies that come out of our mouth: *I won't be long. I'll be right there. Just a minute more.*

Aunt Madeleine was fifteen when she told my father she wouldn't be long, just another minute, and she'd open the bathroom door. My father was a child, a five-year-old; he'd been left alone with Madeleine while their parents crossed the West Virginia line, north into Pennsylvania. They were going to Pittsburgh. Their father went to welcome his soldier brother home from the war. Their mother went to make sure he didn't welcome any pretty young girls.

There were other sisters, three of them: younger than Madeleine, older than my father. Where were they when Madeleine locked herself in the bathroom? This is my father's story, and he doesn't know. He knows the hollow noise a fist makes when pounding on a bathroom door. The pain in the bowels from resisting the urge to push. The smell of bleach – so overwhelming nostrils burn and eyes water. He knows blood smeared on a toilet seat, blood soaked into a white towel. The bulge between Madeleine's legs, under her skirt – another towel. The tiny steps she took, shuffling, pushing from her knees instead of her hips. A knitting needle in her fist.

Madeleine said that she was on fire. She wanted to lie down. She wanted cold water poured between her legs. She told my father that if he stood on a chair he could reach one of the Mason jars on the top shelf of the pantry cupboard. *You can reach one, Paul Edward,* she said. *Stand on your tiptoes and stretch. Fill it up with cold water and pour it on me.*

I see her now, Aunt Madeleine.

I see her in my father's house, perched on a step stool in the kitchen, one slim leg crossed over the other. There are gold chains around her wrists. Her initials stamped in gold on a brown cigarette case. Her hair is red, she's done it herself, she does it to others in the basement of the Doddridge County Home for Little Old Ladies. Old ladies in wheelchairs are brought to her, and she promises to make them pretty. She puts them in her chair and swivels them around. Her foot cranks up the chair. Her slight weight lifts their breakable bodies. It is work, prettiness. It is combs and curlers and heat, and it is bleach. It's my head in a sink, my neck

Shared and Stolen

stretched, revealed. Aunt Madeleine's fingers in my hair. *Tell me if the water's too hot.*

Strands of hair are in the sink. Clumps of hair fall to the floor. Down the back of my sweater. Aunt Madeleine's Cinnamon Honey fingernails snag against my sweater when she brushes off the hair. She sweeps it up and throws it away.

Pretty girl.

I give her fifty cents – a tip, like my mother instructed. Aunt Madeleine drops it in a jar with the rest of her tips. At the end of the week, change will be counted and rolled and given to my mother. Room and board: Madeleine pays her way.

Even on a Saturday night when there are men willing to buy a pretty redhead a shot of whiskey, a pack of cigarettes, a room for the night, Madeleine pays. She's got dollar bills up her sleeves; she pulls nickels out of her ears. She snaps her fingers, and there is a quarter in her palm. If you lock her in the trunk of your car, she'll slip a bobby pin out of her hair, split it between her teeth and get herself out.

Sweet Paul Edward, the other sisters say. *Taking that Madeleine in the way he does.* These are the same sisters who teased my father. They called him *Titty Boy*. Their mother nursed him for a long time. They shook their fingers at him – *Shame, shame* – and they laughed when he buried his face in his mother's shoulder, shy.

His mother didn't want to be pregnant again.

All those babies.

First a girl. Then another. Then the one who lived only long enough to emerge from the womb. Then the one who was dead in the womb – they had to reach in and pull her out. The forceps branded red dents on her temples. Two more girls. Miscarriages, three of them.

Then Paul Edward.
Her boy, my father.

His mother nursed him for a long time. His mouth on her breast saved her.

The flesh hanging between his legs saved him: his father loved him differently from the rest. His father said, *If you women don't put him down, he'll never learn to walk.*

But it was Madeleine he loved the best.
Madeleine who left and who came back.
What did she look like back then?
She was a pretty girl.

She'd be a pretty girl if she'd crack a smile once in a while. This is what my mother said about me.

Smile, so I can see those dimples, my father said. *I want to stick my finger in them. I want to see how deep they really are.* He touches my face; I can smell his breath. Pipe tobacco. Beef jerky. Whiskey.

Never marry a man who has four older sisters, said my mother. It means that he's had five mothers. It means that every time he stretched out his arms, a woman has been there.

What about the daughter of such a man?

Shared and Stolen

What happens when she is there?

Not a woman, but a girl. Her body has years to go before hair will grow under her arms and between her legs. Before breasts swell under her sweater. Before she has to hang her stained panties on the inside clothesline. What happens when this man stretches out his arms and this daughter is there?

> I know what happens.
> This is my story.
> There is nothing I can't tell you.

I can tell you about the boys who loved me. Bare-chested boys in the summer time, white tee-shirts hanging from the back pockets of their jeans. They left bunches of wild daisies between the screen and the front door. They stuck bouquets of weedy little flowers in the mailbox. They sent me songs over the radio. My father said, *There's the fox, and here come the hounds.* He said, *Get me my gun.*

But they were unrelenting, these boys. They were the greasy rainbows in puddles of oil at the end of the lane. They were the cigarette butts in the bushes beneath my window, the ashes on rose petals. My father's dogs barked at them, nipped at their feet. Their feet climbed the trellis; their hands pressed against my window screen. When I kissed them through the screen, their mouths tasted like dust and metal. *Come out, Sylvia,* they said. *Don't be afraid.*

I'll be right there.

Just a minute.
I won't be long.
I was lying.
But not because I was afraid.
There was someone else I was waiting for.

I can tell you about the house my father's father built, in a hollow, this house, made of criss-crossed logs. My grandfather struck down trees with an axe. He whipped the horses that skidded his logs. He had sawdust on his clothes and in his veins. He passed it on to my father. There's the church that Grandfather built. There's the board fence he put up to keep others from hunting in his meadows. The cemetery he's buried in is on the slant of a hill – this keeps rain from flooding the graves. When I stood on my tiptoes, I could see his headstone from the screen in my window.

From my window, I could see tree trunks painted white. Red circle tacked to a round bale of hay. My father's hunting clothes – forest camouflage, fluorescent orange – swinging stiffly on the clothesline. The boxes where dogs on stakes paced, beating dirt circles around rusty stakes. The yellow dog tore into the ground, bringing up pieces of colored glass, a cracked milk bottle, the handle of a teacup.

In this house, a woman gave birth.

In her marriage bed, she pushed out a baby. Bleach soaked the blood out of the sheets, but not out of the mattress. She flipped the mattress over and gave birth again.

A daughter ran away from this house.

Shared and Stolen

My father returned to the sink, again and again, filling the Mason jar with cold water. Outside, the sun was hot and the dogs were howling. Madeleine was screaming. She wanted to spread her legs, keep them open, allow moving air and flowing water to cool her. My father pushed her legs together; he wanted the bleeding to stop. Beaded water rolled across the hard wood floor. My father lay down, in the water, the blood, beside his sister, stroking her hair and sucking his thumb. He fell asleep.

When he woke, Madeleine was silent. Mrs. Hilyard was standing over her. Broken jars of preserved fruit – peaches, blackberries, crab apples – sticky on the floor. Mrs. Hilyard said, *Paul Edward, where does your mother keep her mop?*

She said, *Where can I find a bucket?*
She said, *Don't tell me what happened here. Don't tell anyone.*
Three days later, Madeleine ran away.
Where did she go?
If you ask her, she'll say, *My lips are sealed.*
She was seventeen when she came back home.

Golden hoops in her ears.
Scar tissue on her womb.
She didn't bleed monthly anymore.
While she was away, she learned how to shape and style and cut hair. How to make hair grow long. How to make hair grow thick. How to grind flower petals and tree roots, add a few drops of bleach, and change the color of hair.

I'm back, she said.
Why did she come back home?
Where else would she go?
She's going to leave home someday, said my mother to my father. *Get used to it*.

Sit with me, said my father. He hooked his thumbs through my belt loops. *So sweet. Such a pretty girl*.

Sweet and pretty and eight years old. I was a dainty girl, tiny bones. My mother taught me the difference between a salad fork and a desert fork. I broke my bread before I buttered it. I wasn't a tall girl, but I carried myself as though I was, always feeling my mother's stiff fingers poking between my shoulder blades. A stern woman, my mother. *Straighten up*, she warned. *There are things I want for you*, she said. She twirled a piece of my hair around her finger, stretched it across my cheek and under my nose. She curled her fingers around my ears.

I see her with my father in the cemetery grass, her fingers curled around his ears, her mouth tugging on his bottom lip. She loves him. She brushes saw dust out of his hair. In his face, she looks for pieces of her own: spaces between front teeth, wide eyes, a cleft chin. *You're so spoiled*, she chides. She's ten years older than he is. He wants a son, but it took her body thirty-eight years to make a daughter. There are deep lines etched around her eyes. *Crow's feet*, says my father.

This is about a woman's body: not the one in the cemetery grass, but the one that no longer wants to be touched. My father says, *You're no*

Shared and Stolen

different from your mother. He means the hair that hangs to the small of our back, our crooked pinky finger, the mole on our inner left thigh. He means the strength on our legs. *How fast can you girls run? Let me chase you.*

Who does he catch this time?

My mother. He can make her do what he wants.

My mother. She left, but she didn't come back.

She disappeared in pieces: a lump in one breast, a lump in the other. It spread.

In the kitchen, my mother, one foot propped on a step stool. Her knife chops dimes out of carrots, half dollars out of cucumbers. She says, *There once was a woman who asked the chef at the Waldorf Astoria to give her the recipe for his Red Velvet Cake. He did, but it cost her three hundred dollars. That woman got even. She gave out the recipe, and each woman she gave it to passed it on to another. I'm giving it to you.*

My mother points to the white spots on my fingernails and says each is a lie I will tell. *Some will be necessary.* Each is a boy who will love me. *Many, my baby.* Her womb is shrinking. Her ovaries harden. She doesn't bleed monthly anymore. She gives me a plastic spray bottle with a squeeze trigger and says, *Mist water on me.* She opens every window in the house. Dust settles.

One morning, my mother washes her hair, rinses it with vinegar, and lets it dry in the sun. She lets me run a wide-tooth comb through it; I twist it into a braid. We go to the Doddridge County Home for Little Old Ladies, and she tells Madeleine, *Cut off my hair. It's too heavy. I need to feel lighter.* I watch Aunt Madeleine stretch out the braid and snip. I watch my mother disappear.

She's gone, buried beneath the cemetery grass, and my father takes me to the woods. He pulls up a root and says, *This is ginseng. It makes people love you.* He touches a shiny three-leaf plant and says, *This is poison ivy. It doesn't affect me.* Along the stream, we find a nest of six wild duck eggs. My father says, *I'm taking these.* Back at the house, he arranges them in an incubator.

On this night, my father reaches for his wife, but she isn't there. In his dream, she lays in her nightgown on top of the sheets. Her eyes are closed. She says, *Here's what's left of me.* He runs his finger down the length of her nose. She says, *In the cellar, hanging next to the garlic, you'll find a braid of hair.* His hand rests on her neck; his fingers tighten. She says, *Go to sleep, Paul Edward.*

On this night, my father dreams of rescuing his wife, but she won't be saved. He wants to take her away from the doughy-faced man whose lungs are blackened by coal dust and whose liver is soaked with white lightning. From the tattooed man with a crew cut who claims he won her in a game of darts. *Come home, Madeleine,* he says. He holds out his arms, but she won't come to him. She says, *Take yourself home, Paul Edward.* She turns away. The heels of her shoes are as narrow as the strap of her purse.

Shared and Stolen

On this night, my father enters his daughter's bedroom.

This is not a dream.

He sits on the edge of her bed. His fingers trace the petals on her pillow case.

His fingers slide down the length of her nose. He wakes her by parting her lips.

Wake up, little sister. Sit with me a while.

He stretches out his arms and I am there.

Pretty little girl. I'll keep you safe.

The crumb of sleep in the corner of his left eye.

The taste of the blackberries he'd eaten. The whiskey he'd swallowed.

He said, *I can show you how much I love you.*

This happened.

I can tell you that it happened to me.

Every day for twenty-eight days, my father turned those eggs. He stroked the pointed tips of them, gently, with his calloused thumbs. He pulled the shade of a lamp and held one against the bare bulb.

What do you see, Sylvia?

I saw the shadow of his fingers through the shell.

Five eggs hatched wet bony creatures. Naked, pink. Their bills snapped open wide. My father kept his ducklings wet in the oven; he filled my wading pool so he could teach his ducks to swim. Three sank because their soft feathers didn't bead off water. Another didn't know enough to paddle. But one duck could swim.

In my bedroom. My father said, *Give me a smile.*

The ducks roosted in the bed of my father's pick-up truck. They pushed against the screen on the front door when they heard his voice in the kitchen. He tore hunks of bread from the center of a fresh loaf and they climbed over each other to eat from his hand.

They loved him.

In the middle of the night, his vision blurred by whiskey, my father stumbled over a pile of ducks. He kicked at them, and they scattered, noisily. But they came back. He sat on the front porch swing, sipping from a mayonnaise jar, chewing on his pipe, and they settled on his lap.

But there was one egg that didn't hatch. Cracking it opened revealed a fleshy gray mass. Maybe there was a bill, webbed feet, but maybe not.

Aunt Madeleine said, *Let me show you how to save yourself.* She held a needle in the blue of a flickering match; she held a chunk of ice against my ear lobes. The rhinestone on her ring pressed against my cheek as she forced the needle through my flesh. *Tell me if it hurts.* She inserted one tiny gold hoop, then another.

> *Look at you*, she said.
> She said, *Pretty.*
> She said, *Learn to use it.*

This is the summer I turn fourteen. My father catches me sneaking a sip from his mayon-

Shared and Stolen

naise jar. He said, *That stuff'll pollute you, little sister.* He caps his fingers with shot glasses and says, *Match me. A punishment to fit the crime.*

Clear liquid from a mayonnaise jar is hot. It burns my nose, my throat, a slow burn in the tips of my fingers, at the ends of my toes. But I can match him, again and again. It doesn't affect me. He passes out on the front porch swing, cheek to knees, a cigarette dried between his lips and ashes on his feet. I enter his pockets: twelve dollars and change that I don't take.

It's not enough.

The summer I turn fifteen. He catches me in the woods on the faded cloth seat of a rusted chassis long abandoned, covered only by the sawyer he'd hired the day before. Three shots fired at the sky. Three counts for the naked skinny boy to run from angry dogs.

A poor boy. His pockets were empty.

There's a patch of red, seeping bumps spreading up my arm. It's an itch felt through my skin to deep in my bones. Poison ivy. My father says, *Here's how to get rid of that.* Striking with a vent brush, he rips open my skin. Pours bleach over my bloody arm. A crusty scab forms.

My father says, *You'll grow new skin.*
Pretty skin, pretty girl.
Learn to use it.

Aunt Madeleine says, *I had a father just like your father. He loved me so much he almost killed me. Once, I didn't know I was still alive. Once, I wanted to die. My little brother saved me, but who will save you?*

She says, *You will.*

My father says, *Let me show you how much I love you.*

My mother said, *Some lies will be necessary.*

I said, *I love you, too.*

I knew how to make him weak.

I learned to use it.

Aunt Madeleine gets me a job at the Doddridge County Home for Little Old Ladies. I wear a white blouse tucked into a white shirt. White shoes. My father teases me. He says, *Here's the bride, but where's the groom?* I change diapers. I change narrow beds and soak the sheets in buckets of bleach. I give old ladies in wheelchairs plastic baby dolls; they rock them in the crook of their withered arms and hum. But one old woman grabs her baby by its yellow hair and hurls it across the room, angry.

This is Mrs. Sampson.

I like this woman.

Ninety-seven years old, Mrs. Sampson has the disease that lets you forget. Her spotted hands drift past her face, but she doesn't recognize them. She concentrates on the white walls, the black lamp, the shadows. She says the teeth in her mouth don't belong to her. She says the women who work here are whores. She doesn't know the man who comes on Sundays to comb her hair. He calls her *Gram.* He says, *She has pretty hair, don't you think? Your aunt wanted to cut it short when she came here, but I wouldn't let her.* He stands behind his grandmother's wheelchair, gently stroking her hair

Shared and Stolen

with a soft-bristled brush. He says, *She used to do this for me.*

On my knees in Mrs. Sampson's bathroom, scrubbing the toilet, I watch him with her, wrapping her hair around his fingers. She sits, silent. He runs his hand through her hair, brings a bunch of it to his nose and inhales.

That's when I knew: this is who I've been waiting for.

I could make him come to me.

I could make him do what I wanted.

When he sees me, he calls me *Miss.* He says, *Miss, can I move her chair so she can see out the window?* He says, *Miss, she's been holding her pills under her tongue and spitting them out.* He says, *Miss, what's this I hear about strange men giving you girls money in a room down the hall?*

I say, *I can show you that room.*

His grandmother sits in her wheelchair, facing the window. I stretch the divider curtain across the room so the patients and nurses and visitors walking by can't see me kiss him.

It was that easy.

It always is.

This is about a daughter.

Not the girl whose brother doused her with water from a Mason jar.

Not the girl whose father's fingers parted her lips, whose father's finger tasted of blackberries.

This is about the daughter who slipped money from a man's wallet, pulled money from the pockets of his pants while he slept.

It doesn't happen in the house her grandfather built: not in his bed or her own.

Not in the cemetery grass.

Not in the woods, along the stream.

Not even in the man's truck, on the soft leather interior.

Her feet over his shoulders.

Her hands in his hair.

She can see the clearing where her grandfather cut, and where, thirty years later, her father cut again.

It might've happened there in the truck, but it didn't, because this is when he says, *look at the print on the windshield.* He says, *Take your shoes off. I want to see if your toes match those prints.*

I could have been a fairy tale princess; instead, I was a thief.

I emptied his wallet, the pockets of his pants, in a motel room on a Sunday afternoon.

He fell asleep with his hand tangled in my hair, his breath moist on the nape of my neck. My arm dangled over the side of the bed. His pants, slumped on the floor within my reach; in his pockets, change I didn't take, three crumpled fives, a twenty, bent at the edges. In his wallet, behind his driver's license, two crisp hundred dollar bills. My white clothes – child bride, nurse's aide – neatly folded and piled at the foot of the bed. He stirred, whispering, *Where are you going?*

I won't be long.
I'll just be a minute.
I'll be right back.

Carnegie Mellon University Press
Series in Short Fiction

Fortune Telling
David Lynn

A New and Glorious Life
Michelle Herman

The Long and Short of It
Pamela Painter

The Secret Names of Woman
Lynne Barrett

The Law of Return
Maxine Rodburg

The Drowning and Other Stories
Edward Delaney

My One and Only Bomb Shelter
John Smolens

Very Much Like Desire
Diane Lefer

A Chapter From Her Upbringing
Ivy Goodman

Narrow Beams
Kate Myers Hanson

Now You Love Me
Liesel Litzenburger

The Genius of Hunger
Diane Goodman

Slow Monkeys & Other Stories
Jim Nichols

Ride
David Walton

Wrestling With Gabriel
David Lynn

Inventing Victor
Jennifer Bannan